S0-FQW-545

JUST FOUR CATS

Sandra Harknett

Just Four Cats

Copyright © August 1999 Sh Presentations/ Sandra Harknett
First Printing 1999

ISBN: 1-884687-23-7

All rights reserved under International Copyright Law. Contents and/or cover many not be reproduced in any form, except for the inclusion of brief quotations in review or article, without the express consent of the Publisher.

These are true stories and no substitute names have been used. All four cats are still alive and well, residing with the author at the time of publication.

ACKNOWLEDGEMENTS
(in alphabetical order)

Joe Bionci for encouragement, help and for always being a friend; Marge Caldwell for prayers when Snowball was missing; Bill Dionisio for his friendship and for placing the first book order; Chris Dorer for being a good friend and neighbor (and for allowing her picture to be used); Professor Steve Drabik for editing and suggestions; Rev. & Mrs. John Esposito for prayers; Duncan Ewald for getting me started and for motivation; Rich Harknett, my husband, for allowing me the freedom to pursue my dreams; Ellen List, my sister-in-law, for encouraging words; Bill & Patty Piergionvanni for leading me to the saving knowledge of Jesus Christ; and Rev. & Mrs. Bill Stiles for grounding me in Biblical principles in the beginning. Thank you all and may the Lord bless you.

Published by: New Horizons Publishing Company
P.O. Box 1601, Bloomfield, NJ 07003

Scripture quotations are taken from the NIV/KJV Parallel Bible Copyright © 1985. All right reserved. Scriptures marked (KJV) are taken from the King James Version. Quotations marked (NIV) are taken from the HOLY BIBLE NEW INTERNATIONAL VERSION. Copyright ©1973, 1978,1984 International Bible Society. Used by permission of Zondervan Bible Publishers.

Cover Design is an original drawing by artist Nora Vlack Healy.

Printed in the USA

DEDICATION

To my mother and step-father, Frank and Dorothy Gadzia, whose loving tolerance of all my childhood animals, ranging in size from a skunk to a horse, enabled me to develop a deep rooted love and compassion for all God's creatures that has lasted me a lifetime.

To my daughter, Jennafer Arnold, who was responsible for bringing home our first two fur children. Had it not been for her doing so, there wouldn't be a book today.

To my extraordinarily special friend, Nora Vlack Healy, (the cover artist) for all her hard work and words of encouragement. She has been my biggest fan.

And in loving memory of my father Wilber H. List

*I acknowledge the Lord Jesus Christ
as the source of my life. I thank
God for the inspiration, the
strength, and the resources to write
this book and to see it through to
completion.*

JUST FOUR CATS

CONTENTS

Windy's Story

In the Beginning

Birds, birds, birds. Birds everywhere! Blue, green, yellow, lavender. I started out with just one pretty blue parakeet named Josie, and ended up with a house full of parakeets, one of almost every color. They fascinated me with their little bird antics, and I was intrigued and delighted by the rainbow of hues that they were clothed in. I loved to watch them as they bobbed up and down on their perches, making happy bird sounds (to them, I presume, it was singing) or when they played with their make-believe friends, who usually were bells or other objects sold for the amusement of these little, multi-colored feather-fluffs.

In the beginning my little flock lived in an extra bedroom in our house, so in actuality I didn't have a whole house full of birds but rather just one room full. Most of the time I left their cage doors open, so they had free access to the room. Occasionally they flew back and forth across the room, but for the most part they liked to just sit on the curtain rod and peck the wallpaper off the wall. As a fun hobby this pastime greatly surpassed everything they had thus far encountered in their unpretentious existence. It was pretty funny to see them stretch as tall as they could on their little toothpick legs to remove the wallpaper. Just as an artist uses the strokes of his brush to create his masterpiece, daily they used their little beaks to create their own masterpieces. The artist in them was undaunted. Whenever the canvas became boring or out of reach, they simple moved over or onto another curtain rod and creatively continued. The cream colored wallpaper with golden flowers above the curtain rods was systematically removed and replaced with picturesque dips and peaks, as the bare white of the wall was revealed. They danced around and chirped with glee as each petal and stem floated to the floor.

The humor ceased one day when I was planning to invite a new friend for an overnight visit, and I recognized what a total disaster the "bird room," alias guestroom, was. It was an appalling sight and I realized that it no longer was a guestroom suitable for people. I'm sure the birds were very proud of their artwork. To them the nicely scalloped, bare wall edges all around the curtains were utterly charming, giving the room a nice homey, lived in look, but to me it was a frightful mess. They had discreetly taken over the room without my realizing it, and destroyed it. Well, maybe the entire room wasn't destroyed, but the walls were certainly defaced beyond repair. My potential guest was a very prim and proper elderly lady, brimming with the elegance and refinement of generations past, and I winced at the thought of her staying in that room. *I winced at the thought of anyone staying in that room.* It was not a pleasant sight and I wondered how its offensiveness had managed to escape revelation until now. Since there was no urgency for this visit to take place, just something I had in mind that would be nice at some point, I decided to relocate the birds (to where I was not sure) and redecorate the guestroom. My mind and thoughts became totally consumed with how I would restore this hideous bird habitat back to a bedroom worthy of gracing the pages of *House Beautiful* magazine.

Two of the flock—Adina & Timmy in the dining room

About a week later, and after much thought, I moved the birds into the dining room where they were confined to their cages. Since they were birds, they probably could have handled the cold turkey withdrawal of their freedom without any adverse side affects, but I relented and allowed them out of their cages for about half an hour every day—*under strict supervision.* I called this their "free-fly" time. This was the best I could do to help them make their transition from a life of raucous freedom to a caged existence. Believe me, during this half-hour they were very closely watched, because even though they were tiny they still were an adeptly swift wrecking crew once they got started. I didn't want the dining room instantaneously ending up to be a disastrous mess like the bedroom did.

We're really not the type of people who do formal entertaining, so the only guests we ever had were our parents or a few close friends. I didn't think any of them would mind dining with a bunch of birds. As it turned out, no one seemed to mind at all, and if anyone was disturbed by the bird's presence, no one said so. As I said, they were confined to their cages most of the time, so it was not as if they were flying overhead as you ate.

> *It was a terrible little creature—seven pounds of fight and fury . . .*

My dad actually said he liked having the birds around. When he and my step-mom would visit from Ohio, he would sit at the table long after we had finished eating and watch the birds. He called it *Bird TV* and said he'd rather watch them than some of the stuff on real TV.

The birds had all settled into their new quarters and life was peacefully settling into a spring time loll. Nothing lasts forever, especially those serene times in life. This particular tranquil moment in time was abruptly concluded when my daughter brought home a stray cat. It was a terrible little creature—seven pounds of fight and fury all dressed up in a pretty tabby and white coat! How could such a cute little thing be so nasty and angry? What possibly could a cat have to deal with to give it such a loathsome attitude? Having a cat never entered my mind since we already had all the birds, but if I did want a cat I was certain it would not be this one. This cat was not safe for human contact. Your hands and arms were swiftly shredded if you picked it up. I couldn't understand why Jennafer would want this horrible little beast. Surely there had

3

to be a nice, friendly stray cat around somewhere that needed a home. Apparently there wasn't, and this was to be the cat if we were to have a cat. Actually, that decision was never made as I recall. It just stayed.

She (we decided that it was a female because there was no visible evidence to prove otherwise) stayed outside and my involvement was limited to adding cat food to the grocery list each week. My daughter and her friend Chris had a paper route, and the cat made the rounds with them. Actually, on this paper route is where the cat first made its appearance, and as Jennafer put it, "She just followed me home." Right. How many parents have heard that sad story? She was a cute little cat and I could see her appeal, as long as you followed her "look but do not touch" rule. She was a tabby with perfectly marked little white feet, a white bib, and a white splotch on her nose. It looked as if she had wandered too close to someone painting and got some white paint on her face. She had the typical tabby spots on her stomach, which I thought should be petted whenever she rolled over and showed them off. But in her mind they were only to be looked at and admired and never, ever to be touched. I found that a hard lesson to learn and kept breaking her number one rule. I may still have scars somewhere to attest to my thick headedness over this matter. I still think that pretty spots on stomachs should be petted.

The cat really liked to be with people, just as long as it was on her terms. Previous descriptions of her behavior have convinced you, I'm sure, of the risk involved in trying to touch her—you were definitely taking a real chance with keeping your body intact. My main concern, however, was keeping my precious, pretty, little birds in one living piece, so I viewed this new addition to the family with uneasy trepidation.

I decided not to worry because if she did venture into the house there was Bogy to deal with. I thought this would be a sure deterrent to her wanting our house to be her house too. He would surely show her that this house belonged to him and the birds, and, oh yeah, the people too. Her location was outside and she had better stay out of his way and out of his house. That was a lovely thought on my part but that was not to be the case. The cat recognized him as being big, but not that big. His authority could be challenged. A piece of cake. She charmed him with her cat ways and when that didn't work a simple swat would put him in his place. Bogy was our German Shepherd and it only took one of her left hooks, equipped with dagger sharp claws, to teach him not to mess with her. She whacked him good on the end of his nose one day, and one bloody nose was enough for him. The best he could come up with was to pounce at her every now and then when she turned to walk away. However, in some strange way they did eventually form a bond of friendship, because the day that Bogy died, it was Windy who stayed with him on his dog bed to the end. Yes, Windy, that's the name Jennafer gave to this little monster-cat. Jennafer said the name had something to do with the fact that the weather was very windy the day she found her. I always thought it a strange name for a cat.

Chapter 2

Kittens?

E very summer my daughter would go to visit her grandparents and her aunt and uncle and cousins in western Pennsylvania. While she was gone I continued to feed the cat. I had owned cats as a child but this was not a cat to me. Cats were supposed to be sweet, soft, lovable things. Real pets. This was not a pet. Not to me. So when she ended up missing for a few days it didn't phase me a whole lot, although I did feel bad for Jennafer because she did view Windy as a pet. During one of our phone conversations, I told her the cat was missing. I wanted her to adjust to the fact that perhaps the cat would not be here when she returned. During the next conversation, I told her the cat was back. It ended up being a one-time disappearing act on Windy's part, which subsequently has not been repeated, not even for a day.

We presumed her to be about ten months old when she arrived, so now she would be about a year old. She had been gone for three days. Some of you cat people might know what it means when a cat is missing for about three days. If you don't know, you might get your first clue in about sixty-four days when a bunch of little cats (kittens) arrive. Yes, Windy was away on a mating rendezvous and returned home in a family way.

B A B Y   W I N D Y

We were in the clueless group and were surprised and enlightened in sixty-four days when five kittens magically appeared. I had noticed a tomcat in the area that was mostly white with black spots, and from the looks of the offspring, he was the father. One kitten was black and white, one was gray with white spots, two looked like Windy—one was almost an exact replica of her (we called it "Baby Windy"), and one was an all gray tabby. She gave birth in my daughter's bedroom, the logical choice, since that was the only place in the house where she

Windy with her five, little, newborn surprises!

"The Kittens" at four weeks old

was allowed to be because of the birds. Oh yes, the birds. The excitement of all this new life in the house had momentarily caused me to not see the whole picture. Then when I remembered we had birds, plus now too many cats, my heart skipped a few beats and then started racing. Six cats in the house with six birds was a sobering thought. What if these cute little fur balls turned out to be like their mother? If all six of these monsters of destruction ganged up on the birds they could overturn the cages, bend the bars apart, and have bird hors d'oeuvres for a mid-afternoon snack. My imagination went wild and came up with an almost endless list of possible atrocities they could perform collectively as a group. Immediately I started asking everyone I knew if they wanted a kitten. Jennafer, of course, suggested we keep one. What kid is there that sees kittens and doesn't want one? I suggested she totally forget that idea and not push her luck. One cat with a house full of birds was one cat too many in my estimation.

Now enters Augel into the story. "What is an Augel?" you are asking. Augel was a little, all black, four-month-old kitten who just happened to appear one day, also on the paper route. My daughter was on a real roll attracting stray cats. He also was brought home. If she would have put as much effort into collecting the newspaper payments from the customers as she put into collecting cats, her papergirl career may have lasted a little longer than it did. I recall her non-lucrative papergirl career grimly ending after I had made about a month's worth of payments, paying for the entire neighborhood's newspapers. Of course, in her eyes, the entire endeavor was well worth it; she didn't make much money but did gain two cats out of all her hard work.

Augel produced the loudest purr that I had ever heard come from a cat. It seemed to reverberate from his very heart and it somehow touched a chord in my own heart. My birthday was approaching and, when it arrived, I was officially given Augel as my birthday present from Jennafer. Very clever on her part.

Nice homes were found for all five kittens; we did not keep one. Jennafer made the decision that Augel would be our kitten and ensured his permanent future with us by giving him to me as a present. He must have been pretty special to waltz right into our house in the midst of five newborn kittens and become the chosen one. Somehow he remained as they moved out and on.

Windy had been a good mother, but once was enough, so shortly thereafter she was spayed. We had that little operation originally in our plans, but nature caught us unaware. We thought she was still too young to become pregnant. Obviously, my cat knowledge was very limited at the time. Being a mother had been a positive experience for Windy and she had lightened up ever so slightly in her attitude. The first time I ever heard her purr was after she had given birth to her kittens, and even after they were gone she would occasionally be pleased enough about something to start purring.

I don't recall there ever being any serious situations between the cats and the birds. Augel was to be our house cat so when he was still small we taught him that it was a big "NO-NO" to go near the birds. He was not even so much as to look in their direction. This one thing he did seem to learn. Windy, on the other hand, had to be watched every minute. Most of the problem with her bothering the birds was eliminated because she usually stayed outside in the daytime and slept with Jennafer at night. Augel stayed in my room with me at night—after all he was my birthday present. So this birthday cat became my cat, more or less, for the time being anyhow. As time marched on, the bird problem was totally solved. My fascination with them had somewhat waned, so as they died off they were not replaced. They are wonderful little pets but I decided to be a cat person for awhile. I'm sure one day I will once again have a feathery friend or two because they are beautiful and delightful pets.

Chapter 3

Up Trees & Under Cars

Jennafer and I would try to visit my mom and step-dad in Florida every winter for about a week. We were blessed, at that time, to have a wonderful neighbor named Ellen to take care of our pets whenever we went away. Through the years, she has tolerated many animals. The largest number of animals she had ever taken care of at one time for us was six birds, two cats, and a dog.

Upon our return home from one of these visits, we were welcomed back north by an intensely heavy snowfall. We arrived home from the airport late that night, so I didn't go to visit the cats in the basement where they both were indisputably relegated when we went away. I was tired from the flight and just wanted to go to sleep. So that's just what I did; I went to bed. However, shortly after I had fallen asleep, something or someone banging on my bedroom window suddenly awakened me. Our bedrooms are on the second floor and not readily accessible, so this was a little alarming to me. Outside my bedroom window there's a small slanted roof which is the top of the porch. I opened the curtain to see what was banging on the window. I saw something but I wasn't sure what kind of a something it was. It was an animal of some sort with about two inches of snow on it. All I saw was a snowy mound with two eyes transfixed on me. It wasn't a big animal and it was really very comical looking, but still the experience was a bit eerie. I was still groggy with sleep and I was not quite sure what to do as it kept banging at the window. Then I heard a barely audible "meow." I recognized that meow. I said, "Windy?" Yes, it was Windy. Poor thing! Immediately I opened the window and let her in. She had somehow managed to sneak out of the basement and Ellen wasn't even aware of it. Windy is a very sneaky—or more politely put—clever cat, so this didn't surprise me at all. She had to climb a fairly large pine tree and then jump onto the slanted roof and crawl up to the window in order to pull this stunt. Personally, I thought it was very smart and resourceful of her. I could picture her reasoning it all out in her mind before she attempted it. She was cold and outside. We were warm and inside. In order for her to get warm she had to get inside. The people were not downstairs by the door to let her in, they were upstairs sleeping. She would have to get upstairs somehow in order to get in, and that is just what she did. Yes, I'm sure she thought the whole thing out very methodically before she tried it. She was the smart cat. Augel was the...well...let's just say he wasn't the smart cat. In his story you'll find out a possible reason why he may be a little on the mentally slow side.

Windy decided that this was a new permanent way into the house, and we had to eventually trim the tree to prevent her from getting onto the roof. Trees grow back, however, and being so smart she kept an eye on it. As soon as the branches were long enough, she was back up it. My mind drifts back to an incident that happened one time when my parents were visiting and staying in the now very lovely guestroom. My mom was adjusting the mini blind before she went to bed and was scared half to death when she saw a hairy thing hanging on the outside screen of the window. I told her to calm down, it was just Windy. Mom was still startled. There's a street light on the pole in front of the house that plays a major part in this scenario. When Windy would want in, she would hang on the screen spread-eagle style, and with the light behind her she would make a big frightful looking shadow on the wall.

To discourage her from thinking that this particular window was her own personal entrance, we finally had to stop allowing her to come in the window. Most of the time when she showed up at the window, we did not want her in the house, not to mention that she was destroying the screen. She would just appear at the most inopportune times and we wanted to put an end to it. So instead of permitting her to come in through the window, I would go outside and 'call her down.' It was not as much fun coming down the tree as it was going up because there were a lot of dead branches and the pine needles were sharp, so she eventually stopped doing it altogether.

Another year or so had come and gone and we were once again making arrangements for Jennafer to go visit our relatives in western Pennsylvania. Her dad and I were extremely busy at this period in our lives, and it was good for her to be going to where she got the attention that she deserved. Life's busyness can suck you into the whirlwind of no return if you are not careful, and that's what happened to us. My biggest mistake, since moving from Pennsylvania to New Jersey, was that I became too busy for things involved with the church and God-related activities. Previously people would describe me as being very religious; I would describe myself as a Christian, convinced that there is a difference. Religion is man reaching up to a god, trying to be good enough to deserve favor. Christianity is God reaching down to us, all we have to do is accept His provisions. Things that had no lasting value took up all my time. Ironically, those very things that were so important then served no purpose in my life and aren't even a part of it today. My "too busy for God, do my own thing" attitude lasted for several years. Foolishly, I had detoured off the straight and narrow path, but God in His faithfulness saw to it that my road, the wrong road, once again crossed His path and He gently nudged me back in the right direction. Forgetting God and doing our own thing does have its cost. It cost me a marriage, but fortunately not the deterioration of a little girl's innocence or self worth. Children also can get way off the path or come up with some strange ideas when not enough time is given to them, but God faithfully watched over Jennafer even when I was too busy to do so. For that alone I am eternally grateful to Him. Nowadays if I feel myself getting too busy for God, I know that I am just too busy—and adjustments are made in my life *tout-de-suite*.

My parents live a little over six hours away, but as I said we were busy people, so we usually made airline reservations for Jennafer's trip. I honestly don't remember how she got there this particular time, but my mom and stepdad were driving her back. They lived in Florida in the winter and were heading back south by way of New Jersey in order to bring Jennafer home. They were due to arrive late in the afternoon and then we were all going out for dinner.

Windy must have been hanging out at someone else's house when they arrived because she was not around. She was now a very social cat and would go to wherever she heard people. She had become an extremely friendly little cat (on her terms only, of course) and was well liked by most everyone. By now she knew everyone in the neighborhood and even followed the mailman for several blocks as he made his daily rounds. As we were driving up the street, returning from dinner, I noticed Windy across the street in the park. We pulled into the driveway and when Windy saw Jennafer get out of the car she raced across the street right in front of a car! She was hit head on. We all heard the heartbreaking thud. Jennafer screamed an awful earth-shattering shriek. She just kept screaming, "My cat, my cat, my cat." Several of our neighbors dashed out of their houses to see what had happened. The driver of the car stopped and apologized, saying that the cat had just appeared, seemingly out of nowhere. He was so sorry. We knew. It was not his fault. Surprisingly she was not instantly killed, as we assumed, but rather she flew out from under the car and kept moving. She ran up our driveway and vanished behind the house into the bushes somewhere. We looked everywhere for her. Several neighbors, my parents, my husband, Jennafer, and I all searched and searched to no avail. Sadly enough, I said that she probably just went under a bush someplace to die. We'd find her in the morning if we could. We all felt just awful. We had all heard the impact of a big car against a little cat's fragile body. It was hard to get the sound of the thud out of your head. I tried to put it out of my mind but I just kept hearing the tires screech over and over. A joyful homecoming suddenly turned into something unbearably sad.

Even sadder yet is the fact that I was too preoccupied with busyness to even think to pray about it. But I'm sure Jennafer prayed for her cat that night, hoping it was her turn for a miracle.

I worked for a newspaper at the time and left for work around 5:00 a.m. My main concern at that hour was to get up and get myself awake and moving. The alarm would go off at 4:15 a.m. and I would be just going through the motions of a person awake until I got into the car; that's when I officially woke up and began my day. So the next morning when I stepped outside and saw Windy sitting on the top step it took me a moment to realize the significance of that. When it dawned on me she was supposed to be dead, the shock of it zapped me wide-awake. She had an annoyed look on her face because she must have thought we forgot to bring her in for the night. There was not a mark on her. I quickly took her upstairs and woke Jennafer and gave her her cat. Jennafer was deliriously overjoyed, but I cautioned her that although Windy appeared to be fine she could possibly have internal injuries and still be hurt very badly. I wanted her to be prepared for the worst, but thankfully the worst never happened. As far as Windy was concerned, the whole thing was yesterday's news and she could barely remember it. That's Windy. Our neighbor George has been calling her a "very durable little cat" for many, many years. I looked up the definition of durable in the dictionary and it means "lasting, constant, impervious, tough, and enduring." That she is and has been now for eleven years!

Chapter 4

Round And Round She Goes

D ay after day after day I heard water running someplace in the house. I was constantly checking the faucets and the toilets but nothing, apparently, was running or leaking. I couldn't understand what the problem was, and the constant distraction of it was making me hover near the edge of mental derangement. A couple other aspects about this situation bothered me too: why didn't anyone else in the house hear it, and furthermore, why didn't anyone else seem concerned about it? I was torn between whether I should ignore my family members, as they were ignoring my water problem and me, or react with violence towards them, accompanied by loud outbursts to get their attention. As I said, this was making me a little crazy. I looked at the water meter in the basement and it was not moving, so that should have settled it, but I *knew* I heard water running.

As I went down the basement stairs with a laundry basket full of dirty clothes, I stopped midway on the steps as I was once again met with the sound of water running. *Again* I checked all the possible sources and found nothing. I had had it with this. I stomped upstairs and called the Water Department and told them about my small time crisis. They listened (unlike anyone else) and said they would send a man to check it out tomorrow morning. Wonderful! I was happy now. Peace and contentment replaced my frustration and it felt good. I happily bounded back downstairs to continue my laundry session. As usual, my daughter had washed clothes and left them in the washing machine. This usually was a cause for instant rage, but on this particular occasion it didn't bother me. The waterman was coming and I was happy. I took all her clothes out of the washer and put them into the dryer. Just then, the doorbell rang. I went to the side door, and a gentleman announced that he was from the Water Department. Wow! Talk about expeditious. This Water Department is really on the ball. He said he got the call and already happened to be in the area, so he thought he'd take a chance that someone might be home. Was I home? I had been here for weeks waiting for someone to take this problem seriously. He came in and *he heard water too*. I already really liked this man. We immediately bonded, a kindred spirit type thing because we both had the ears it takes to hear running water, not in my house, but outside *under the street*. That's what the problem was—the city's water pipe in front of our house had a leak in it. The tree in front of our house had been recently removed. Actually it had fallen on the house, and when the city workers removed it the roots had somehow damaged the water pipe. As the tree was pulled out the roots probably tugged on the pipe and caused it to spring a leak. This was just great and I was overjoyed to hear about it, in spite of the fact that it was creating a massive problem for the city. He said that when they dug up the water pipe it would make a big mess in front of our house, but I didn't care—the water would at last stop running. That's all I cared about, stop that vexatious water running!

I bounced back down the basement steps to pick up where I was with the wash. I loaded up the washing machine and started it, and then I closed the door on the dryer, started it also, and headed back upstairs. When I got to the top of the steps, I realized that something was banging around it the dryer. I didn't recall Jennafer having anything bulky, like tennis shoes, in with her clothes. Sometimes the lint catcher would come loose and it would make a clunking noise. That must be it I thought. Back down the steps. When I opened the dryer door, to my horror, Windy staggered out, looking dizzy and dazed. Fortunately the dryer did not have time to heat up to the degree where she got overheated. This was one of those awful, awful situations that you don't even want to think about anymore after it is over. All I'll say is that I hope she would have started making some kind of noise to let me know she was in there if I didn't come back. If she didn't, well . . . as I said, I don't even want to think about it. (I'm sure the heat would have suffocated her.)

So that was the day Windy tumbled round and round a few laps in the dryer and used up number two of her nine lives. The expression "Curious as a cat" must have been coined for cats like her. She'll try to get her inquisitive, little cat body into any miniscule crack, tiny spot of space, or anything left open to see what's inside. And she never learns. Many times at our house she's been shut in drawers or closets and trapped in the garage. As she wanders the neighborhood, your guess would be as good as mine as to how many other places she has found herself stranded. Knowing Windy, I'm sure there have been homeowners who have closed doors to sheds or garages unaware that a curious little busybody was inside.

After Windy had her kittens, and also had her operation to insure that she never would have kittens again, the father of the kittens would still hang around. Sometimes we'd come home at night and they'd be sitting on the front steps together. I began to feel a deep respect for this tomcat. Perhaps it wasn't just a one night thing and he genuinely liked, or could it be, loved her? That's what I thought. However, sometimes there'd be several tomcats outside with her. Now what was going on? I mentioned this to the vet when we took Windy in for her routine shots, and she said perhaps when Windy was spayed (the operation was done elsewhere) that a piece of her ovary was left and it was still making hormones that would attract male cats. She suggested a blood test to confirm this idea. That's exactly what the problem turned out to be, so poor Windy went under the knife again to be spayed a second time. You can imagine how shocked I was to see that this still did not solve the problem of all the cats congregating at our house. I'm not really sure what the problem is (it still exists) but my understanding is that she has an excess of a certain hormone or hormones that attracts male cats. Then when they come they seem to have no idea what they are doing here, so they all just sit around making those outrageous cat noises at each other. And Windy doesn't have a clue either. Sometimes they chase after her and she either runs away or swats at them, but that's about it. The vet said we could give her medication to counteract this problem, but Windy would become a lethargic medicine head and not the endlessly energetic cat that we know and enjoy. We opted to let her be. Who knows, maybe she does just have a lot of friends and there's nothing more to it than that.

Chapter 5

Loving Life and People

Windy has an endless amount of energy and believes that this whole world, or at least our back yard and as far as her little white feet will transport her, was created just for her enjoyment. I have never seen her pass up an opportunity to have some fun or to play. A leaf gently swaying in the breeze, any and all moving insects, clumps of dirt, and innumerable things unseen to the human eye, all these and more, are her fascinating playthings. She's not one for catnaps, but rather is awake all day amusing herself. When there are no moving objects to attack or pounce upon, she creates her own games. One of her favorites is the "Sixty-Second Dash." She invented this game herself, and although I have never seen the official rulebook for it, from watching her play it I think it goes something like this. The goal is to run as fast as you can for sixty seconds up the nearest tree and then turn around and back halfway down in quick, choppy, plummeting movements, only half way—I know that's one of the important rules. Then you daringly jump the rest of the way, landing, of course, on all four feet. As you get better and faster at it, you end up higher in the tree and consequently the halfway point jump is also longer and thus more daunting.

Strangely, she couldn't interest any of the other cats, our own or the strays, in playing this game with her. So she plays it herself almost daily and the lack of cat enthusiasm from the other cats doesn't seem to matter to her. The other game, in which she also finds herself the solo player, is the "Walk the Fence" game. Our fenced in yard has a dangerous fence with ragged wire edges on the top of it. She walks the entire length of it, placing her feet between the protruding wires, until she reaches the end. Thereupon she rotates around and walks the length of the fence to the other end. Without any exaggeration at all, I counted her doing that eight times one day, back and forth, back and forth. I even pointed it out to my neighbor who stared incredulously at what this strange little creature was doing.

Although I'm sure there are many, many more ways that she amuses herself which I am not aware of, I do know of this one other game she plays with unsuspecting passersby. She strategically positions herself under the bushes in front of the house. Although there isn't an extraordinary large amount of foot traffic on the sidewalk, there is enough to keep her busy. A small convenience store is located just around the corner on the next block, so she uses the people on route to it as her pawns. As the unaware individual approaches, she crouches down in her hideout under the yellow cypress bush, and then leaps out and attacks their feet. Feet are moving targets, perhaps deadly, which need to be dealt with whenever possible. I'm sure that is how she sees it. It's only the feet that she is concerned with. One day, it must have been a visitor, not a regular, because the poor elderly lady jumped up and down doing an impromptu version of an Irish jig while making peculiar noises. Windy regularly does this pouncing, attacking of the feet thing to my feet when I am in the backyard, so I know it's all in fun—her claws are never out. It's just a little startling when your mind is lost somewhere in a daydream. The regulars in the neighborhood know her, so after she has had her fun, they usually stop and pet her. She'll permit, out of learned politeness, a few strokes on her head, maybe a scratch behind the ears, and that's it. Stick around too long, or try to pick her up, and she turns into this little wild beast. She has retained the same antagonistic attitude that she showed up with the first time I ever encountered her. That's Windy and that's how it'll always be

Someone, a man, did try to carry her off one day. He picked her up and advanced only as far as two houses. Then I saw him abruptly drop her. I also saw him looking regretfully at his hand and arm. I'm sure she demanded to be put down by showing him her ten very sharp claws and a full set of healthy teeth. Jennafer was just getting ready to open the window and yell, "Hey, that's my cat. Where you going with her?" Before Jennafer even got the window unlocked, Windy as usual, had handled it herself. Since some subconscious part of her must really want to be a friendly cat, we have been concerned about someone stealing her. She's always out front socializing with people. However, since we've seen her in action when this *"be my friend"* thing is taken too far by people, we've stopped worrying about her. Although only eight pounds, she is well able to take care of herself.

The only time I can remember Windy not having endless energy was several years ago when I would repeatedly get those chronic, annoying, wintertime illnesses. I'd be home from work sick in bed, often for a week or more, usually with an earache or bronchitis. Windy would sleep on the bed with me and never venture away. This tender attitude was not characteristic of her, but I welcomed her thoughtfulness and found it endearing. In retrospect, it seemed that I was besieged with illness during that period of time in my life when I had put

God on a shelf. Not being blind to the fact that good, God-fearing people do get sick and even die, I do, however, still believe that Jesus died not only for our salvation, but also that we may walk in heath under His protection. My favorite way to phrase it is, "God puts us into a blessing bubble." For me personally, since I have been back on the straight and narrow path, God has blessed me with perfect health. I no longer succumb to the winter ills that Windy saw me through. Actually, she hasn't even so much as taken a nap with me in the bedroom since that time. Our bedroom is just not one of the places she regularly frequents, but apparently when I needed a friend during rough times, she decided she would be the one to fill the need.

From Windy I learned that life can be fun if not taken too seriously, neither it nor yourself, and much, actually most of what we get rattled about isn't even important a day later. One of my favorite sayings is "This won't matter in a hundred years." Along the same line, one of my favorite scriptures is "What good will it be for a man if he gains the whole world, yet forfeits his soul? Or what can a man give in exchange for his soul."(Matthew 16:26 New International Version) *That's what will matter* in a hundred years. None of our accomplishments, our degrees, our prestigious titles, or the list of the important people we knew, no, none of that will be on our tombstone when we die. Hopefully we can leave some faith and values to live on in the lives of the people we have touched with our own lives when we are gone.

As for Windy, I'll remember her for as long as I live because she is one unique cat with one extraordinary attitude about life. Although she is twelve plus years old at this writing, she has not slowed down at all. I'm sure she'll be around for a long, long time yet. After all, she's only used up two of her nine lives!

End

*Hiding
in
Leaves*

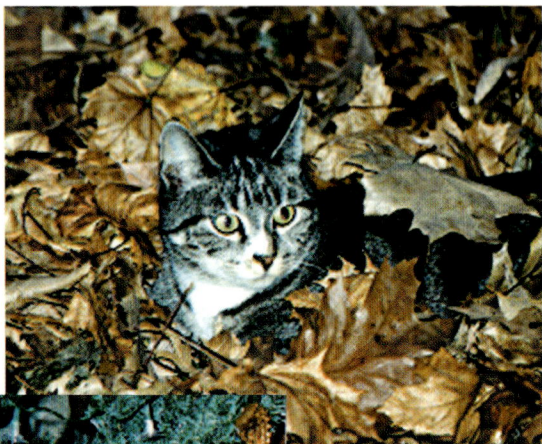

**C
H
R
I
S
T
M
A
S
!**

*Windy
at
Play*

*Squished
in a
Shoebox*

22

Jennafer
&
Windy
Through the
Years

July
1987

September
1990

August
1998

23

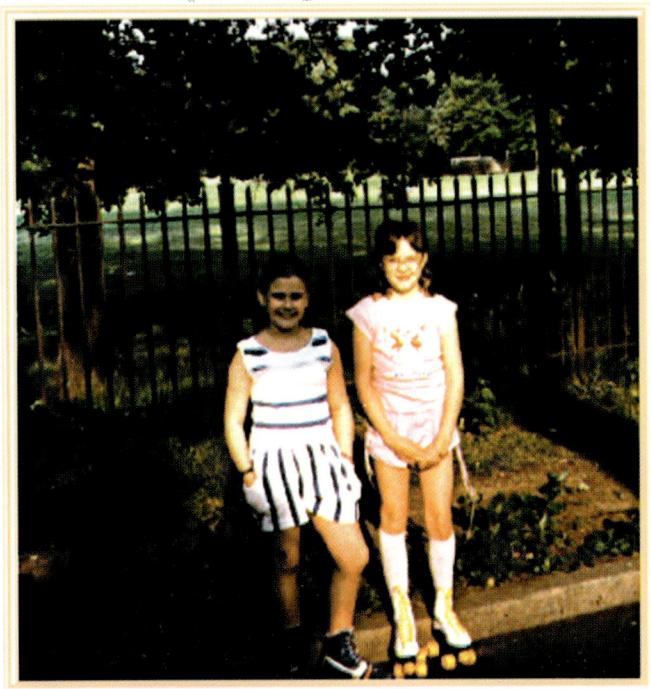

Jennafer & Chris—co-finders of Windy in the 80"s and in 1999

Windy

Augel's Story

No! No! No!

I worked in the circulation department for the largest newspaper in northern New Jersey at a job that I loathed most of the time. Although I felt I was paid very well, I also felt I was more or less trapped in this situation because of my financial obligations. I worked my way up from a part-time delivery person to, what they called, the Zone Supervisor of an entire town. I was up at 4:15 a.m. (yes, morning time) and was usually finished and back home by 1:00 p.m.—truly an enviable hour to be finished with work by most people's standards, but I was so exhausted that most of the time it didn't matter. Although my official job description included a number of responsibilities, it seemed like my sole responsibility was to make sure that all the newspapers, thousands upon thousands, were delivered—everyday. When we were short people, or employees just didn't show up, the job of doing the actual delivery fell upon me. Sometimes I would deliver hundreds and hundreds of papers day after day, week after week, without any days off. I finally was offered a better job at another newspaper, and on my exit interview I was told it was a shame I was leaving because I was next in line for a promotion. I didn't say anything, but I thought to myself, wow, I would have been promoted from delivering papers everyday to delivering papers everyday. You see, everybody delivered papers when we were lacking people. That's the name of the game. It doesn't matter how wonderful your newspaper looks or the terrific editorial content, if the paper doesn't get to the customer all that is meaningless.

It was after one the above mentioned abominable and exhausting days when I first met the subject matter for this story. I pulled into the driveway, got out of my car, and dragged myself to the front door. At that time our house had a lovely screened-in porch on the front of the house. That porch area has since been converted into my office, actually the very office where I now sit writing this story. I unlocked the door and headed in only to be met by a shoebox filled with cat litter and two small bowls, one with milk, one with food. This present assortment of cat conveniences could only mean that something extra, probably looking a lot like a cat, must be lurking somewhere on the porch. "Meow, meow." It appeared vocally first and then bodily, seeming very happy about at last having some company. It was a little black kitten about four months old. I was not in the mood, and try as he did, he could not project his happiness with the situation upon me. Our cat, Windy, who recently had joined our family uninvited, had just produced five kittens. My exhausted body was silently functioning in a stupor, but my wide-awake mind was screaming, "No, no, no." I promptly put *little black cat* back outside and sent him on his way. Surely it had to belong to someone and they would be looking for it. That was that. I had no feelings of sorrow for the cat, no feelings of pity, no feelings at all. I was exhausted and needed my half-hour nap. I went to sleep and he went, well . . . who cares where he went? Looking back I can't believe that I possessed such a callous attitude toward a tiny, innocent, helpless, little kitten. It must have been the ink in the newspapers.

Jennafer was rather understanding about my sending her new, little friend on his way. After all, we already did have a house full of cats. That was a relief—there was to be no scene over having yet another cat. It seemed to have disappeared, so not another thought was given to the little creature.

My husband had a second job and usually arrived home around 10:00 p.m. He had been home for only a short time when we heard a very loud animal sound coming from outside.

> *I promptly put "little black cat" back outside and sent him on his way. Surely it had to belong to someone and they would be looking for it. That was that.*

We went out to the front yard and realized that it was coming from a cat stuck at the very top of the pine tree located at the side of the house. Not just any cat. Of course, it was the little black kitten. Apparently, he had not gone very far when I sent him on his way. He went all of about twenty feet horizontally and then twenty feet more vertically—straight up the tree. We had to get the ladder and my husband climbed up the tree to get the little cat down. He handed the kitten to me and it started purring the loudest purr that I had ever heard come from a feline. What an utterly incredible purr! Windy was not a purring cat. She just recently had started to purr ever so softly, and only when she was with her kittens. I loved the sound of the little guy's purr. I wondered how he could create such a loud sound. I was in awe. Obviously, I was a bit more rested and better equipped mentally to deal with this second appearance of him than I was the first time around. I don't think even his outstanding purr would have impressed me earlier in the day.

> *He went all of about twenty feet horizontally and then twenty feet more vertically—straight up the tree.*

Jennafer was only too eager to resurrect his shoebox litter box. It was put out by the garbage earlier, so she hauled it back onto the porch. The porch seemed to be a good place for him to stay until we found his owner, or a new home for him. We offered him some milk and he drank so much that I honestly thought he would explode. He looked like one of those over inflated balloon animals on a stick that you buy in the checkout line at grocery stores. I thought for sure he had ruptured something internally and was going to die. Apparently not, because he just kept purring away. I kept wondering how such a deep rumble could come from not much more than a handful of fur.

No one in the neighborhood seemed to be missing this little black kitten, which Jennafer had already named Lucky. As I previously mentioned, and if you read Windy's story you will remember that at the time of this black kitten's appearance Windy had just given birth to five kittens. They were still practically newborns when he arrived. Jennafer had expressed a strong desire to keep one of Windy's kittens, and I had expressed an even stronger desire that this was not my desire. She came up with what she thought was a very good compromise, a winning deal for both of us. This unbelievable good deal for me was if I would let her keep this newcomer, she would not want one of Windy's kittens. Talk about not getting it. I said, "Listen Jennafer, what part of *NO* don't you understand? This already is a *no-cat household* with one cat in it. One thing we absolutely do not need is another kitten, no matter what size he is, or how cute he is, or how loud he purrs." Yes, that purr—it was outrageously, but endearingly loud. As said so well in Windy's story, it seemed to reverberate from his very heart and it somehow touched a chord in my own heart. "Well, Jennafer, I'll think about what we'll do with this little augel", was my compromising reply. Augel. What's an augel? I truly have no idea; it was just a word that came out and seemed to sort of fit him. I didn't like the name Lucky, so without any more thought or discussion given to it, he became Augel.

Augel—November 1987

My birthday was approaching, and when it arrived, I was officially given Augel as my birthday present from Jennafer. Very clever on her part. I guess she thought she could get away with this because I did just absolutely adore his purr. She rightly presumed that he had won me over somehow. So our no-cat house now became a two cat house.

If he was to be our cat he would have to be a housecat, thus avoiding all the bad things that can happen to cats outside. Augel also thought that this *housecat only* idea was great because it was November and it was starting to get cold outside. However, this wonderful idea we both (Augel & I) had did not abide well with Windy. After all, she now had a family to protect, and couldn't understand the reason for his staying, already knowing that there couldn't possibly be any purpose to bringing into the house yet another cat. Hadn't she done her job and supplied us with enough kittens? Was there really a need for yet another one? She definitely thought not. Although we tried to keep them apart, growls and hisses were exchanged every time they had a chance encounter. Probably this new confrontational situation between the two cats was a major factor in Jennafer's decision to give him to me. "Let mom work it out," she thought.

Augel was more than happy to sleep in my bedroom at night, so that at least solved the nighttime problem. In the daytime, Jennafer would keep the door to her room, where Windy and the kittens lived, closed. So at least for the time being, the problem was solved.

Prior to Augel's arrival, we had planned on visiting my in-laws over the Thanksgiving holiday. This presented a problem because we could not allow Augel to be alone in the house, even though Windy and her kittens were permanent residents exclusively in Jennafer's room. We could not confine him to the basement, because he was just a little guy and there were far too many things down there that he could have gotten into and perhaps even injured himself with. Hummmm, what to do? My husband decided that we would take him with us. After all, it was his parents that we were visiting, so if he thought it was an okay idea then it must be. I never did fancy my mother-in-law as being a cat lover, or a lover of any animals as far as that was concerned, so I did have my doubts as to whether this was a good idea or not. In any event, the three of us, Augel making four, packed up and headed to

Maryland, which was about four to five hours away. We humans each had a suitcase and Augel had a litter box, a blanket, and his food and water supply.

He slept almost the entire trip and didn't even seem to be aware that he was traveling anywhere. He was only a kitten, so what did he know about what life was supposed to be like. This car ride thing could be normal as far as he was concerned. He had warmth and comfort and food—was there more to life than that? He didn't know yet so he would just sleep until he found out.

As I recall, his arrival was a surprise to our hosts, but they were cordial about it and decided that one small kitten could not be that much trouble. A little home away from home was set up for him in the basement, and he was, as my mother-in-law put it, "the perfect guest." You didn't even know he was there. We added that to our list of things to be thankful for on Thanksgiving. It could have been a very long and unpleasant weekend if he had acted up or messed up or ruined anything.

If you have ever traveled any distance for the Thanksgiving holiday and then attempted to return the following Sunday, you will know what a nightmare the trip can become if something happens to disrupt the flow of traffic. Well, something did happen on our return trip on the already infamous (only when there are events to disrupt the flow of traffic, otherwise it is wonderful) New Jersey Garden State Parkway. There was an accident and the traffic completely stopped for several hours. A helicopter had to land on the parkway to take the accident victims to the hospital. It was a very sad and tragic end to someone's holiday. The return trip took us over eight hours, but for Augel that was just twice as long to sleep. He curled up under the front seat and slept, once again, almost the entire trip. We had a little litter box for him, but he did not feel the need to use it. That also was added to our list of things to be thankful for on this Thanksgiving.

All and all it was a pleasant but uneventful holiday getaway. I thought of spicing up the story with some made up incidents of suspense and intrigue, but then that would spoil the whole book, which is entirely true. The main point to be gleaned from this incident is that cats can be good, trouble-free traveling companions. Perhaps from Augel's Thanksgiving Day adventure, someone else could be persuaded to take their cat on vacation or visiting with them. That is, if your cat is like Augel and likes to sleep anywhere, a lot. I think he was just thankful that we took him along and didn't leave him home alone, and we were thankful everything went well.

Chapter Two
The Cost of Never Forgiving

T he next problematic situation that arose concerning Augel was indirectly Windy's fault. She had been a furniture scratcher whenever the opportunity was available to do so. Even when she was just passing through the living room on her way to the basement, or to Jennafer's room, she would deliberately get a couple of good scratches in on the end of the couch, before dashing off at full speed. She knew this was not allowed, and she let you know that she knew she was not allowed to do it by the look on her face as she did it. It was as if she said, "Ha, Ha, look at what I'm doing. Catch me if you can!" So . . . if we were to have a cat in the house, it would have to be declawed.

The next cat to come was to be Sylvester, and if he had been there first, there would never have been any declawing of anybody. Sylvester is perfect in all ways and would never think of using any of the furniture as a scratching post. But alas, he had not appeared on the scene yet, so poor Augel was declawed.

Today I believe with proper training and other devices to distract cats from clawing the furniture, that declawing is rarely needed. In contrast, we were still very new to cat ownership and was told this was the thing to do to prevent our furniture from being destroyed. Windy's defiant behavior enforced our conclusion that all cats with claws will destroy furniture. If I would have briefly paused and thought back to my childhood, when it seemed that I always had a kitten, I would have realized that none of our cats had ever used the furniture as scratching posts.

In later years Augel did use the ends of the chairs and couches to simulate sharpening his nonexistent claws, so perhaps in the end, for him, we did do the right thing. As you read on you'll see that he also became an apartment dweller at one point in his life. His lack of claws worked out well for this situation too.

Poor little Augel came home from the vet with his front paws in bandages and wanted to be comforted by someone of his own kind. These seemingly nice people with a warm house and good food had caused him pain and unhappiness. He wanted his closest thing to Windy; she understand. She and they could language about pain. He Jennafer's room

> *Even sadder, for the brief moment he was in her domain, he saw kittens which made him want to be in there even more.*

mommy. The it for him was would was a mommy converse in cat his betrayal and hopped over to the best he could on his bandaged toes, pushed the door open, and proceeded in. POUNCE KER-BAM!! He was brutally attacked by Windy. Poor Augel, who was now a very defenseless creature, was instantly ousted from the room. Even sadder, for the brief moment he was in her domain, he saw kittens which made him want to be in there even more. He had brothers and sisters like them not too long ago and wanted a better look at them. He boldly attempted reentrance into the room. Once again he was expelled, but only after a small, but serious altercation.

To this day, many years later, Windy and Augel do not get along. They only tolerate each other's existence. When they are in an intolerant mood, which is often, they pick up right where they left off on that very day. Personally, I've been saying for years that Windy hates him because she thought he was going to hurt her kittens, and Augel hates Windy because she made him try to defend himself and he injured his toes. Yes, I forgot to mention, his little bandages were all bloody when he at last emerged from Jennafer's room. When Augel only wanted to be comforted, Windy caused him immense and unnecessary pain. He hasn't forgotten and hates her for it. And she returns this feeling of animosity towards him.

May I interject here, that their behavior is a very good example of how we, as loving Christians, should *not* act. We've all heard people say, "I've forgive, but I'll never forget." God totally forgives and forgets all our sins and iniquities, and that is what he wants us to do. Maybe it's a good thing for me that Windy and Augel are around to regularly remind me how *not* to act. Sometimes I wonder how different and more enjoyable their lives would be if they would just be friends. I guess it's the same with some people. Their lives could be more pleasant and enjoyable if they would just get over and forget about being wronged or mistreated by someone else. The Bible says not to let "any root of bitterness" start growing within us. When we do not forgive, we feed that root and it grows into an ugly monster within us causing nameless problems, emotional and physical. I've heard of chronic illnesses abating when people have let go of bitterness and unforgiveness towards someone or something. Windy and Augel spent more than ten years together. They could have been good friends. When I see pictures of other people's cats curled up together, sleeping peacefully, or sitting side by side looking out the window, I can't help but sadly ponder what could have been. Windy and Augel's existence could have been so much more enjoyable for them.

From a cat's point of view, if they reason things out—and they do appear to from time to time—, you can understand Windy's additional hostility toward him when she saw each of her precious little babies given to new homes, yet he remained. "Why was a new home never found for him," she wondered.

Later on a spraying war would erupt all over the furniture in the living room, trying to prove who was top cat. He grew to be exactly double her size, weighing in at sixteen pounds, whereas she remained at her top weight of eight pounds. However the weight difference didn't matter. The war raged on and on. Windy was smarter and quicker and Augel was just bigger. All said and done, Windy was usually the victor by employing simple but cunning strategies. All she would have to do is jump up on something higher than Augel and he didn't have a clue where she went. One of her favorite tactical maneuvers was to jump up on the chair in the dining room, which was naturally located under the dining room table. A true no-brainer, but Augel never thought to look there for her although he saw her disappear under the tablecloth before his very eyes. When the battle progressed upstairs, a quick dash under the bedspread would once again stump Augle. He would be clueless as to where she had disappeared. As I said, she was smart; he was just big.

I don't know if he was always, to put it politely, just not as smart as Windy, or if this next incident had anything to do with his, bluntly put, mental dullness.

Chapter 3
Bangs & Bruises and Cuts & Scrapes

It was December of his first year with us and time to start getting ready for Christmas. We store all our Christmas decorations in the basement, so Jennafer and I began bringing armfuls of boxes and bags upstairs. As we rummaged through each new arrival to select our favorite decorations and ornaments, we created a huge mess. Empty boxes and plastic bags were everywhere littering the living room floor. Augel, enthralled with kitten curiosity, thought it was wonderful. He began exploring each empty box and bag until he somehow got his head caught in the strap handle part of one of the plastic bags. He backed up to rid himself of it, but it backed up with him since was around his neck. When he moved, it moved with him. In his mind he thought it was chasing him, so instead of allowing us to simply remove the bag from around his neck, he took off running like a crazed animal all around the house. Round and round he went with the bag flapping at his head. He had himself in such a frenzied state that he started not seeing straight and repeatedly banged his head into the walls and doors. The more frightened he became, the faster he ran. Jennafer was leaping at him with hopes of grabbing him, and I was trying to head him off at the doorways, but over and over again he slipped through both of us. After all, he thought something awful was after him and he had to get away. I'm sure he wondered what we were up to the way we were yelling and running wildly around, but he'd see what our problem was after he out ran this thing. It seemed like an endless chase, round and round and round the house, but finally we did catch him. He was somewhat dazed and out of breath. If we didn't catch him when we did I think he would have saved us the trouble by knocking himself out. He probably could have withstood only another crash or two before collapsing completely. We wonder to this day whether he caused some permanent damage to his brain by all those repeated hits against the wall with his head. So when he acts a little dense, we take this into consideration and just love him more. Maybe he just wasn't too bright to begin with, but that's okay too. Afterward we were a little more careful with where we left empty bags. To say the least, Augel's first experience with Christmas wasn't so merry.

Augel, or Augie as we nicknamed him, matured into a big (all of sixteen pounds), beautiful, glossy, black cat. He was totally black with not a white hair on him. I used to tell him that he had no face, because all that was visible sometimes were two eyes. His black nose and black mouth blended into the rest of his face portraying a black faceless image.

He was always very curious about what lurked through the doors, in other words, outside where Windy went to frolic in the fresh air and sunshine everyday. We were told that once you allow your cat outside he'll want to go out all the time, so it would be best never to allow him such liberties to begin with. That seemed reasonable to us, but not to Augel. Every day, day in and day out, he would attempt his escape. Upon entering and exiting the house we had to exert extreme care in order to foil these relentless attempts of his to break out of the four walls of imprisonment that held him captive. That's no doubt how he viewed the situation, but in reality he, as most indoor cats, had a very comfy and cozy life. For whatever reason, when it was raining we became a little lax about keeping an eye on him. We thought just because we knew it was wet outside, that he should also know that it was wet out there and thus no place a sane cat would want to go. Even Windy came dashing homeward at the first sign of approaching rain.

As fate would have it, he made his first escape in the middle of a tumultuous thunderstorm. He was totally drenched by the torrential rainfall in only a matter of minutes, at which point it must have dawned on him that something was not quite right in this world that he previously thought was a utopia. We watched him drag his soggy little body under an overhang by the basement window where he huddled in a dumbfounded stupor. Someone retrieved him and that was the end of that. Until the next time it rained. When you are rushing into the house with an umbrella, books, or bags from shopping, you are not really worried about the cat running out into a thunderstorm. So this became Augie's *modus operandi.* I think he started to believe that it always rained outside, because every time he had been out there since he could remember, it had been raining. He started to act normal in the rain. Instead of seeking shelter under the basement overhang, he would sit in the middle of the back yard, in the rain, and play with worms or watch the birds. The rain didn't seem to affect the birds, which no doubt reinforced his reasoning about its being the norm. We felt sorry for him so we did start to allow him to go out occasionally when it wasn't raining. At this particular time our neighborhood was a safe environment for the cats. For the most part Augel was happy to stay in the backyard. The yard was fenced in and it took him quite awhile to figure out that he could actually climb up the fence and get over to the other side. So after the first up and over eye opening experience, he would every so often venture over the fence and into a neighbor's yard.

One Sunday morning as I was getting ready to go to church, I looked out the window and saw Augel nose to nose with a stray cat. Augie would back up a step and then bat the other guy in the face with his clawless paw. He was not only clawless, but also clueless as to how you should or should not treat visitors to the neighborhood. We rescued him before he really angered the other cat and got himself into a big fight and got hurt. For whatever reason, he did have this antagonistic attitude about him.

Fortunately he didn't get hurt that time, but he really did have a propensity for injuring himself. If there was a small piece of glass or something sharp anywhere, Augie would be the one to step on it and cut his foot. He came home numerous times with small injuries. I don't think he ever got over his hostile attitude toward other cats either, because often it looked as if another cat had taken a swipe at his face or ears. Augie was always the one who was a little banged up.

One Saturday afternoon we noticed that Augel was still sleeping in the basement, so Jennafer went down to get him to see if he wanted to go outside. He slept on a fuzzy pillow shaped like a bear, so that is where she found him. When she went to pick him up she noticed that the pillow was soaking wet and he was unusually warm. His belly was all wet so she carried him upstairs to ask me why he was sweating. He wasn't sweating, but he had apparently been licking his stomach. I took a look at his wet stomach and I cringed when I saw a big gash right in the middle of it. He felt extremely hot, so we immediately rushed him to the nearest veterinarian hospital.

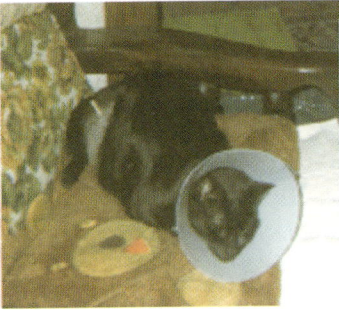

Here's Augie very unhappy in his chair-bed after this misfortunate incident.

Once inside, when the vet started cleaning the wound, we were horrified to see that what had appeared to us as a two-inch long cut started opening up to reveal a nine-inch slash, which took seventeen stitches to sew back together! It was a frightening, take-your-breath-away sight because it looked just as if someone had purposely cut him open like that. It appeared to be a near perfect surgical incision. More bizarre things go on in this world than we like to think about, and I wondered if he was being prepared for some satanic ritual and somehow escaped. A few weeks prior to this a dog's head was seen on the roadside a few streets away. Maybe I have an over active imagination, but he had one grimly perfect, nine-inch incision right in the middle of his stomach. To this day, no logical explanation has been unearthed to explain what really happened to him.

After we brought him home from the vet, he had to be watched around the clock to make sure he did not injure himself further. We had to keep one of those cone devices around his neck to prevent him from licking his stomach or pawing at the stitches. I actually took a few days off from work to be his nurse and to keep an eye on him. We set up a little sick bed for him on a chair in the living room, complete with his bear pillow. His belly was completely shaved to reveal his bare skin, and he had a drainage tube sticking out of one side. His pathetic image was completed with the cone around his head. I'm sure he felt just awful because he just stayed put for several days. All in all, the poor little guy was a very good patient.

Apparently, he had come into the house and just gone to the basement and we didn't even notice anything wrong with him. It was sad to think how he just lay in the basement all alone and suffered silently. I wonder why some animals do not come to us for help when they are hurt. A stray cat that I named Woolly Cat was also always injuring himself. Most of his injuries appeared to come from fights, although once when he contracted ear mites he did allow me to put a prescription cream in his ears. When he was hurt he would come and show me his injuries and I would clean him up and put medicine on his cuts. He would growl and hiss at me the entire time, but nonetheless, he would stand still on his own to be treated. But poor Augie, he just lay there all alone in pain. He quite possibility could have died if he had not been found when he was. He had already lost a lot of blood and had a very high temperature.

After this incident, Augel's roaming days abruptly ended. He had injured himself one too many times and this last occurrence was just too weird. He was allowed outside only when we could be with him in the backyard to make sure he stayed in the yard.

Chapter 4

God's Faithfulness

God always surprises us when we are not expecting Him to do so. He surprised me with a new husband in 1990. Of course, there was a little more to it than that, but I do believe that God sent Rich to me, because he was perfect for me and just what I needed. The cats liked him immediately. Rich has a very nurturing nature, and to this day he worries more about the cats than I do. I actually don't worry about them at all; I just occasionally show a motherly concern. Sometimes when we are on a day trip on the weekend, he insists that we cut it short to make sure that we are home to give the cats their supper on time. I would let them wait an hour or so and not think that it was any big deal, but to Rich it would be unthinkable not to have them eat their supper at the regular time.

It was actually Rich who paid Augel's enormous medical bill when he had his serious stomach injury. Augel was never his favorite, so we endlessly heard about what an expense he had been. I suppose Rich never especially liked Augel because Augel really doesn't have much of a personality; he's sort of just there, just existing. But that's exactly what Jennafer needed, just someone or something to be there for her. That's all our pets really have to do, isn't it? They don't have to be smart, clever, or even pretty; they just have to be there for us. Faithfulness counts a lot.

It was less than a year after we were married that my life was again transformed, but this time in the form of a spiritual reawakening. God will only let you go so long and then He causes circumstances to bring you back. One of the first of many spiritual tests that I was to go through to see if I could retain my new found peace and joy in the midst of trying times had to do with the cats. For whatever reason (it was one of those things only known to the cats that take part in them) Windy and Augel both started spraying—urine, for those of you unfamiliar with cat ways. They started out leaving their special little marks by the fireplace. Then they both decided the brick flooring by the fireplace was a perfect place for their imaginary littler box, which they only urinated in. The real litter box was for the other thing. Every day when I came home from work the puddles would be there waiting for me. We have a very pretty parquet hardwood floor in the living room, and sometimes the urine would run onto that and seep down into the cracks. It was not a pretty picture and definitely not a happy homecoming for me. I never punished them in any way, probably because there's really nothing you can do that they will understand. People who rub animals' noses in their mess should seek therapy for themselves before they try to straighten their pets out by using such barbaric methods. Where that ridiculous but unfortunately common chastisement came from, I'll never know. Animals totally do not understand that type of punishment. I couldn't understand what the problem was and daily went through this very time consuming and expensive cleaning process. I bought special cleaning formulas to remove the odor and presumably to stop them from using the same place. It worked. They got tired of that spot by the fireplace and started spraying the back and the corner of the loveseat. It was a multi-colored floral design, so it cleaned up (daily) fairly well, but it was maddening to have to deal with it everyday. You're probably thinking that by now my house smelled like a neglected zoo, but the odor eliminator product did work amazingly well. Looking back on the entire situation, I would say the problem was a territorial thing between Windy and Augel.

One day I just got entirely fed up with it and said that the cats could no longer be in the house at all. Plain and simple, not to be discussed. That's how it was to be. So they stayed in the basement and only visited us upstairs when we could watch them.

It started out as a lovely day, one of the few weekend days that I did not have to work in a very long time. It was Saturday morning and I was rushing to get ready to go someplace. Somehow Augel had gotten upstairs and was wandering around. Thinking back on it, I recall being very, very angry with Jennafer after this next incident happened, so she probably had allowed him out of the basement and had neglected to watch him. I was in the kitchen, and noticed out of the corner of my eye, Augel strolling into the dining room.

He then stopped by the bookshelf where the stereo was and turned around and sprayed, totally emptying his bladder on my entire cassette tape collection. I screamed at Augel as he was in the process but there was no stopping him. I was enraged. I grabbed the tape containers and started wiping them off as fast as I could. Jennafer heard all the commotion and came running just as I was about to strangle this nuisance cat. That was the day I gave him back to her. I said I'm sorry but I just do not want to spend a large portion of each day cleaning up cat urine. The pact was made with her on that day that if she wanted the cats then she would be the cleanup person. I was finished, through, done; my cat ownership days were officially over.

Silly of me to think that since my cat ownership days were over, that my clean up days were over too. Even though they were exiled to the basement, the marking war to prove who was the top cat went on. Now their favorite place to spray was the washing machine and the clothes dryer. I would go to the basement to wash clothes, and would have to clean up the entire area before I could proceed. Jennafer was in school, so she was no help. I started making her check out the basement before she left in the morning, but it could look fine at 7:00 a.m. and be all sprayed up by 10:00 a.m. It was one of those "I've really had it with things" days when I went to wash clothes and found a very big, smelly mess all around my laundry area.

As I surveyed the massive mess, the timer in my head calculated that I would spend more time cleaning it up than I had spent reading my Bible and praying that morning. Something was wrong here. This endless situation was such a futile waste of time. I had really had it with them and didn't even want to see their little cat faces while I cleaned up, so I opened the door and sent them outside, unsupervised. About ten minutes had gone by and I thought I'd better take a look to make sure Augel was still in the yard. I walked outside in time to see him teetering on top of the fence just before he made his final decent into the neighbor's yard, concluding his escape from ours. Just then, with perfect timing to push me over the edge mentally, Windy dashed by with a bird in her mouth. With catlike precision myself, I sprang into action and with one swift swoop I successfully grabbed her. Although she seemed to be holding the bird gently in her mouth, her jaws were nevertheless clamped shut, seemingly unmovable. However, I became the final victor in this battle with this tiny creature when with much effort I pried her mouth open, as I screamed at her to let the bird go, which she finally did. It was a baby mocking bird. How appropriate—a mocking bird. It seemed as if all of catdom was mocking me that day. One of my hobbies used to be bird watching, when my days were not consumed by delivering newspapers and cleaning up cat messes. Therefore I knew it was a mocking bird because they have those nice, white patches on their wings, which the baby bird flashed at me as a thank you as it flew off. At least someone in the animal kingdom appreciated me. So with the crisis with Windy handled, I proceeded to locate Augel. Of course, he was in the middle of some dense underbrush in the neighbor's yard. I just could not believe the aggravation they were causing me. Jennafer was my only child and she was very easy to raise. She was always well behaved, one of those wonderful compliant children, and these unruly cats made me glad that I didn't have that second, usually defiant child. Defiant cats were more than I could handle, let alone a child. With some prodding, Augel waddled out of the thicket and then played his run all around the house game. I chased him as my neighbor watched in amusement, expressing thanks that he had no pets. I finally did catch him, and don't really remember how that day ended. Somewhere in the midst of it all, it dawned on me to make this a matter of prayer. Surely God could reason with these animals, because I sure couldn't. You know, it actually got better after that day. The spraying never totally ended until Augel moved out, but it did become very rare. Although not really a miracle in the Biblical sense, it sure fell into the miracle category in my mind.

My new spiritual Biblical values did not always sit well with Jennafer. I told her I had to do what I thought God wanted me to do concerning her life and my own life, and that my choices would not always be the most popular thing, or the most fun thing. She went with me to church three times a week, whether she wanted to or not. She often thought that my rules were unnecessarily rigid, but I told her I would have to answer to God someday for how I raised her.

There's one incident that I specifically remember Jennafer and I did not see eye to eye on. One of her young male friends came to visit her at an unacceptably late (very, very late) hour at night. This was after she had received her driver's license and had her own car and she returned home from being "out." I always found "out" not an acceptable place to be, but that was the only answer I received most of the time. This was not someone who had taken her on a date or anything like that, just someone she had met while "out." With my pajamas on, I told him that we were Christians, we read the Bible everyday, and we believed that the Ten Commandments were just that, commandments not suggestions. I continued by saying that the hour he chose to show up was not an acceptable hour for him to be coming to a young lady's house for a visit. His arrival had wakened me out of a deep sleep, and my immediate thoughts turned into immediate words out of my mouth. We never saw him again and Jennafer probably wished she'd never see me again! Someday she'll look back on that event and admit that I was right.

Augel came to live with us in November of 1987 and moved out with Jennafer and into their own apartment in September of 1997. They spent two months shy of ten years together under our roof. He arrived when Jennafer was eleven years old and left with her when she was twenty-one. He remained a constant companion for her, a good friend, and a source of comfort during those sometimes trying teenage years.

In those ten years, Augel saw and experienced many things. He saw the man of the house, John, pack up and leave.

For whatever reason, John decided that marriage, family life, and maybe even cat ownership, was not for him. Varied as the reasons may be, we all do have our reasons to do what we feel we have to do in life. Our lives went on without him. He had many fine qualities and was a good influence on us while he was around, but as I said, life went on once he made the decision to go.

Also during those ten years Augel listened to many, *(many, many, many)* phone conversations that Jennafer had with her friends, smelled much more perfume than his sensitive nose ever wanted to smell, and heard much more loud music than his sensitive ears ever wanted to hear. But he never complained because it was all worth it to him to be near the little human love of his life. I always tried to be a good mother to Jennafer, probably failing as much as succeeding, but today I am comforted to know that even when Jennafer felt unloved by me, Augel was there to make her feel loved and wanted. Animals can do that.

During this time I also had many heart felt conversations with my favorite pet, my dog Bogy. Bogy was another loss that we all (Jennafer, Rich, the cats, and myself) shared during those ten years. I always took him to McDonald's for a hamburger on his birthday, and his thirteenth trip would be his last. At a little over thirteen years old, his life was over. It's said all too often, in many ways, and all too soon—our pets just do not live long enough.

My prayer for Jennafer was that someday she would become so involved with the things of God that her Christian walk would transcend mine and be an inspiration for me. That happened in her late teens. She became very active in youth activities, later a youth leader, and also sang contemporary Christian music in church and in a few local concerts. So again Augel saw some changes take place in the little back bedroom where he hung out with her. The music was still loud, but now it was Godly music and a new peace and joy filled the air.

Chapter 5

Bye-Bye Big Mommy

As I mentioned, in 1997 Augel and Jennafer became apartment dwellers. They moved all of three miles away, although it was to the next town. Augie came back with Jennafer for Thanksgiving (his favorite holiday) the year they left. He had only been gone a couple of months, but Windy hissed at him either in recognition or because she didn't remember him. Either way, it was really all the same since they never did get along. Mysteriously, all spraying had ceased when Augel had ceased to live with us. It was wonderful! However, on Thanksgiving, Windy sneaked upstairs, and realizing that Augel was in residence, promptly sprayed the coat rack, which was located in the living room near the door. They sure had a way of bringing out the worst in each other. After that, we decided it would be best if Augel stayed put in his new home and didn't visit anymore.

Augie in his new home on "his" new water bed

I really had no reason to go to Jennafer's apartment on a regular basis, so sometimes it would be several months between visits. It was mid summer during the following year that I noticed Augel had put on quite a bit of weight. Jennafer would go to the shore almost every weekend in the summer, often leaving on Friday night and returning on Sunday. The blessedness of having a cat is that they can be left alone for several days as long as they have food and water. The problem was that Augel is the type of cat who will eat everything put in front of him, down to and including the last morsel of food. Past experience taught Jennafer that if she left him with his regular allotment of food for three days he most certainly would gulp it down all in one day, probably all in one hour, and would be totally without food for a day or two. To remedy this Augel was left alone with a huge bowl of food every weekend, close to a week's ration, all of which he ate. His gluttony continued until Labor Day arrived and the summer festivities ended. Then he was *slowly* put on a reducing diet. It can be very harmful for cats to lose weigh too fast. His "Big Mommy," that being me, bought him some toys which caused him to run around and jump and play. A little exercise is also what he needed so that aided the slimming process. I was always referred to as "Big Mommy" and Jennafer was "Little Mommy." It was merely a size distinguishing factor; I am four inches taller than she is. It was around Christmastime when I next saw him, and he had definitely slimmed down; he was almost back to the slim and trim cat that I used to know.

One of the things I found humor in was the fact that when Jennafer was at home, she was required to clean the litter box three times a week: on Monday, Tuesday, and Wednesday. For whatever reason this was always a source of big time contention and strife between us. (The Bible says that with strife comes every evil sprit. Something to think about.) We both got very tired of it. I wondered why she wouldn't just clean the insipid litter when she got home from work, and she wondered why it was such a big deal to me when she forgot to do it altogether. The big deal was that Sylvester (number three cat to arrive) would like to go to the basement and use the litter box around 9:00 p.m., before we went to bed. If it wasn't cleaned he would just look at me as if to say, "You're kidding, right? I am not, no way, no how going in there." Then I would scream up the steps for Jennafer to come and clean the litter. This usually was an on-going battle, three times a week: Monday, Tuesday, and Wednesday. Now that she lives alone, ironically, the picture has changed. She not only has to clean the litter on Monday, Tuesday, and Wednesday, but also on Thursday, Friday, Saturday, and Sunday—all seven days of the week. Additionally, she has to buy (pay for with her own money) the cat litter. She readily admits how disgusting the entire apartment smells when the litter is not done daily. Life can be such a wonderful teacher, and we can all be sure that life will do its duty when all else fails. I love it!

One day Augel was very busy in his new home, and his actions could have caused him and the other people living in his building not to have a home at all. As I mentioned, he will eat anything and everything in sight, or in smell's range. He smelled his cat food bag on the counter by the stove and decided it was time for him to have a snack, so he'd just help himself this time. He jumped onto the gas stove, and apparently ignited the burner by hitting the control with his foot when he landed. Fortunately Jennafer was home at the time and took immediate control of the situation. My suggestion was for her to actually put the food in the oven, out of sight where he definitely could not get at it. This worked fine until one day when she was preheating the oven to bake something. You guessed it. She forgot about the food and baked it. It was pretty amazing how quickly it baked and burnt. Unfortunately, it was a new bag of premium, expensive food—totally wasted. I happened by her house that day, and the entire apartment smelled just awful. I decided I would take the food home and throw it in the park for the ducks and birds to eat. That's just what I did, and then let Snowball and Windy outside for a little fresh air. Snowball smelled the food and headed across the street to see what smelled so deceitfully scrumptious. I tried twice to keep him from crossing the street, but he really had it in his head to see what it was in the park that was tantalizing his senses. I decided if he wanted burnt cat food for supper, so be it. He took one whiff of it and dashed back across the street. Evidently something awful happened to it in the baking process and it turned into some really repelling, foul smelling stuff.

Augel has always been a very vocal cat. It's just amazing how different each cat's personality is. Augel would always very loudly demand his food and/or any food that you perchance were eating. Feeding time for the cats was much more peaceful after he moved out.

Sometimes after young adults move into their own apartments, the actual expenses of living alone start to overwhelm them. It was one such time for Jennafer, when due to an abundance of bills that particular week, food was in short supply. She had cooked a steak (the last of her meat) and had taken it into the living room to watch TV while she ate. She got up to get something and placed it on a little table, thus presenting the perfect opportunity for Augel to snatch it and make off with her supper. When she returned, her plate was mysteriously empty. The mystery was immediately solved when she saw Augel in the corner of the room trying to gulp down her steak all in one bite. She tackled him in a frantic rage of hunger, wrestled the meat out of his mouth, washed it off, and continued her supper where she left off. She did cut off the part that Augel had gnawed on and gave it to him, but that was all of it he got. She said it was the only food she had left, and he was not getting the whole thing. Of course, you and I probably would not buy steak if food money was hard to come by, but that's another of life's lessons that experience teaches.

At this writing, which is April 1999, Augel and Jennafer are still in the same apartment. Augle's story was the last story I actually wrote for this book, although it has been placed second to keep the cat's arrivals in sequential order. Our peace and quiet was short lived because Snowball, the fourth cat to arrive, became our new loud mouth cat. Rich has even said that he is worse than Augel was. As I said, they are all so different. Sylvester, our third arrival, never meows loudly or demands food. But he is the perfect cat, so no less would be expected from him.

I could not imagine coming home to a house without a cat waiting for me. We used to have a cat or two waiting on the steps outside when we returned from being away, but now the cats stay inside all day except for a brief time each day when I go outside with them. They seem to realize how much better, and safer, they have it inside, so they usually come back in without much trouble. Augel, on the other hand, has not seen green grass or smelled fresh air since he left; he truly is a full time apartment dweller. He's always there for Jennafer when she needs a furry little friend. That's his main job—to faithfully be there for comfort and companionship. It may not seem to be a very important job in the whole scheme of things, but it really is.

Occasionally we all think that what we do in life is pretty meaningless and unimportant. But sometimes it's the phone call to a lonely or depressed friend, or saying just the right words to someone at just the right moment when they need to hear it, or a small gift given in appreciation. Sometimes we know the effect the kind deed or thoughtful gesture had, and sometimes we won't know the important part we played in someone's life until we see the rerun in eternity. Several years back I had a temp job at a new business in the area. When I decided to move on, a replacement for me was hired and I trained her for a few days. From time to time we kept in touch, and I gave her a Women's Devotional Bible for Christmas that year. That small gift totally changed her life. I was fortunate enough to see the fruits of that particular gift, but often the fruits of our kind acts are hidden from us.

> *God is not always looking for greatness, just faithfulness in whatever it is He has called us to do in life.*

Just as Augel is always there for Jennafer, we need to be faithful to be there for our friends and those not yet our friends. Just being there is often enough. We need not be clever or cute, just be there. The third verse in the twentieth

Proverb says, "Many a man claims to have unfailing love, but a faithful man who can find?" God is not always looking for greatness, just faithfulness in whatever it is He has called us to do in life. All our seemingly small parts in life go together to create the big picture that often only He sees. May we all hear from Him someday:

"Well done, thou good and faithful servant; thou hast been faithful over a few things, I will make thee ruler over many things: enter thou into the joy of the lord."
Matthew 26:21 (KJV)

End

Augel

Jennafer & Augel – September, 1999

Sylvester's Story

Nina

Did you ever crave one certain food and you kept eating it and eating it, and then you ate some more of it until you stopped craving it? Perhaps this over indulgence even made you slightly nauseous. In my case, it often only takes one entire bag of something, such as red licorice, to satisfy this craving. I'll get on a kick with one particular food and over satiate myself with it until I'm totally sick of it, and then I don't want it again for many months, a year, or perhaps never again. I try not to do that any more, but in the spring of 1993 I was craving peanuts (the kind you buy in the shell in a really *Big Bag*) and thus begins this story.

At some phase in your life, if you already don't do it, you may get the urge to start planting flowers in your yard or garden. If you've never had any interest in planting vegetation, chance would have this newfound interest perhaps coincide with the age of forty something. That's what my daughter told me anyhow, when at one point in her life she was studying psychology. This studying of anything must have been a phase (a short one I may add) in her life that she also was going through, but that's another story. I would plant some flowers and putter around in the back yard a little bit, and then get this craving for some peanuts. I'd go into the house and secure my bag of peanuts, the really *Big Bag* that was about two feet long, and bring them outside to munch on while I took a little snack break. I thought the shells would be a good mulch type material for the yard, so wherever they landed after I shelled the peanut they stayed. A strange thing happened each time I brought my bag of peanuts outside. As I started cracking them open, this little squirrel appeared seemingly out of nowhere. When I threw the shells, it would run after them. Then seeing they were already devoid of their contents, it would look at me with the best look of disappointment a squirrel could muster.

Of course—it wanted a peanut. So I shared. Since I had this huge bag, I freely doled out peanut after peanut to my new friend. Surprisingly, it would eat only one or two, and then run off with the third one and bury it somewhere. I still am in doubt as to whether squirrels ever actually remember where they bury their stuff and go back to the exact same location and get it again. I think not. Hence, for two reasons, I started shelling and further breaking the peanuts in half for the little squirrel. One reason being to extend our visit together a little longer. The second reason was to not waste the peanuts. It was just a matter of being practical; I couldn't see every third peanut out of my bag ending up buried in the dirt somewhere.

Since everything that moves in my life has a name, this little squirrel became Nina. I had recently been on an evangelical mission trip to Mexico, and one of the few Spanish words I learned was *nina*. Nina means "girl" in Spanish. Nina was a little girl squirrel, I assumed, because she did not look like the other squirrels in the yard that I knew were boy squirrels.

Nina standing on the picnic table waiting for her peanut.

Yes, I know this is Sylvester's story, but we need to hear about Nina first because in the beginning she played a key part. Nina and I became the best of friends that spring and into the summer. She even came when I called her name. She moved into our backyard, apparently deciding that the company and the food were very agreeable. We have a large pine tree right outside the dining room window, and at the very top of it is where she made her home. This was also a very handy location for her because she would crawl onto one of the branches that almost touched the window and I would open the window and give her a peanut. She became a regular dinner guest outside the dining room window while we dined inside. It was a little startling for visitors sitting at the table to see a squirrel appear suddenly before their eyes while they were eating, but nobody seemed to mind after the initial shock.

As I spent time with her in the yard she became very friendly, and even aggressive about getting her peanuts. Most people would say she only came for the food, but I believe she actually enjoyed my company. She started climbing up my leg to my lap to secure her peanut a little quicker, and even let me pet her little head occasionally. If she didn't like me, she could have stayed at a distance and waited for me to throw her the peanut. I would like to think that she enjoyed our time together as much as I did. After all, life could get pretty boring with only squirrel friends. I brought diversity into her life is how I looked at it.

We had recently hosted a cookout for one of my daughter's friends who was visiting from Florida, and somehow ended up with tons of extra hot dogs. This next incident probably happened a day or so after the party. No, Nina didn't give up her peanuts for hot dogs. Our black cat, Augel (nicknamed Augie), brought home another cat, a black and white stray. They seemed to be buddies. This was during a kinder, gentler time in Augel's life when he was allowed to roam free during the day. After many accidents and confrontations with unfriendly strays, his roaming days have ended. He's currently allowed out only under supervision in the fenced in back yard. This new guy was very, very thin and hungry. To this day I don't know why, but I went inside and got him a hot dog. After all, we had a gazillion of them left

He must have thought that I, like multitudes of unfriendly people before in his life, was throwing something at him to chase him away.

from the party. At first he ran from me so I threw the hot dog in his direction, which frightened him even more. He must have thought that I, like multitudes of unfriendly people before in his life, was throwing something at him to chase him away. I figured if he was hungry he'd find the food later. I didn't

Augie & the new stray cat in the back yard

give it or him another thought. That is until he showed up the next day apparently looking for another hot dog.

This became a daily thing. Sometimes he appeared with Augie and sometimes alone. I cringe today when I think of what a horrendous diet I was feeding him. Today my cats get premium cat food plus vitamins. But it really didn't matter to me at the time what he ate, because from the first time I laid eyes on his mangy carcass, I didn't like him. To me he was solely a garbage disposal to get rid of all those hot dogs. Food is food when you are starving, isn't it?

Week after week he came for his hot dog and became a real pest. He was either scared to death of me and took off at any sudden movement or else clung to me craving attention. Sometimes we crave food—sometimes we crave more important things. I'd have Nina on my lap, since she was the preferred pet of the backyard, and he would jump up onto the chair beside me. This terrorized Nina so badly that she'd take off up the nearest tree. It had been a safe sanctuary for her in our backyard and I was annoyed at this intruder for disturbing our peace. This squirrel seemed very intelligent, but I worried that she would think I had a part in these escapades with the cat. Since I would send him on his way and entice her back, I hoped she was discerning enough to see and understood we both were innocent victims of circumstances.

The hot dogs eventually ran out. Now what? Cat food, what else? He liked that too. He was starving so I'm sure he would have liked anything. More importantly though, I think he liked the small bit of attention he received everyday. He was starving not only physically but emotionally as well. I think I continued to feed him when he came just so he would leave Nina and me alone. Pathetic and needy as he was, I repeat that I really did not like him. We had two cats of our own at this time and they both had green eyes and black noses. One was all black and one was a tabby. This cat had yellow eyes and a pink nose. All his skin was pink, it seemed, even his toes. Our cat's toes were black. Sounds silly, but to me our cats were what cats were supposed to look like. He didn't look right, or should I say, he didn't look the way I thought he should look, so I didn't like him. Isn't that what we do? We judge people because of the way they look or act. Isn't that what prejudice is, having an unfounded attitude already about something or someone (or some cat) without any facts? I caught myself in this mental analysis of this poor cat and why I did not like him. It was solely because of his yellow eyes and pink nose—he didn't look the way I thought a cat should look. I now became the pathetic one. I always prided myself as not being a prejudiced person. I've volunteered one day a week for the last seven years at an inner city Christian School made up mostly of minorities that don't look like me. I had no problem with that. Yet I found within myself the ability to so easily be prejudiced. A cat had to show me that ugly part of me just waiting to come out. Where would it show up next? There are probably attitudes and "stuff" in everybody's life that need to be dealt with. I found something in my life. Maybe this cat wasn't so bad of a fellow after all. I purposed in my heart to be kinder to him. He had feelings too. After all, he couldn't help it if he had yellow eyes and pink skin, anymore than we can help the way we look. Looking back on it, it seems so ridiculous and stupid now but it was quite real at the time and I am not proud of it.

Meanwhile, as I was coming to terms with my own inadequacies, Nina remained in the backyard and lived a very balanced life. She would eat awhile, still take the last peanut and bury it, then go back to work. Yes, she had work to do. She was building her nest for winter at the very top of our pine tree. She would get huge mouthfuls of grass and then trek up to the top of the tree and use the grass for her nest. Once at the top, she would disappear into a huge mound of grass and leaves, so I was never actually able to witness the fine art of squirrel nest building. She spent hour after hour each day going through this same process.

It was by now late summer; fall was soon approaching and Nina worked systematically to accomplish what only a squirrel knows needs to be accomplished before the blustery cold of winter sets in. She would work awhile and then sprawl out on the picnic table, flat as a pancake, for a nap. Watching her methodically balance the activities of her, life, day after day, taught me about balance in life. Do a little of everything that needs to be done, don't over do any one thing, and don't forget to do any of the important things in life. That's balance. We all need it. Too many people get consumed in working to make money to buy and pay for all the "stuff" in their life, but never really have time to enjoy it or the people who are most important to them.

Nina would stay with me for a very short time. That ended up being true in two ways. Each day when she came she would stay only five or ten minutes, although I would see her several times a day. Our friendship abruptly ended one day in early fall when she was electrocuted by a telephone wire on the pole in front of our house. An electrical wire had come down in a thunderstorm earlier in the year, and it was hurriedly repaired leaving exposed wires atop the telephone pole. She was unfortunate enough to bump into one of them and was instantly killed, falling limply to the ground below. I found her in the front yard beside the telephone pole. I knew it was Nina because I had cut the end hairs on her tail straight across in what I called a bob. I had been bitten by a squirrel I mistook for her one day, so I gave her this special hair cut so I could distinguish her from all the other squirrels that frequented our yard. Tears were shed and I buried her in the backyard in one of her favorite places. My elderly neighbor saw me, with tears streaming down my face, preparing to bury her in a little box; he couldn't understand all the sentiment over a squirrel. "After all," he said, "there are plenty more around." More squirrels, yes—more Ninas, no. Once you get attached to an animal it is no longer *just* another animal, it becomes a friend who is a part of you. I missed her a lot. She had actually started to follow me around and spend a little extra time with me when I was outside. She really did like me and not just the peanuts. Maybe she knew our time together would be short. Now it was over. But I still had an extra furry somebody in the backyard that very much wanted to be my friend. I named him Sylvester.

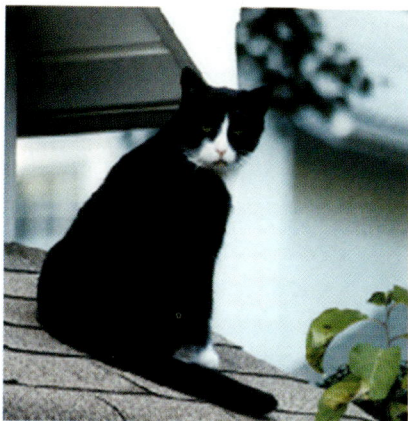

The thought came back to me that at the beginning of the summer I was considering getting another dog. Our dog had died about four years earlier and I was not certain if I wanted another dog or not. One day I prayed and asked God to send me a dog if He thought I should have one. Sometimes stray dogs just wander into your neighborhood and need a home. I thought that would be the easiest way since I didn't know if I even wanted another dog, let alone the type. No dog came, but that was about the time Sylvester showed up. Hummmm . . . .

Chapter 2

My House or Your House?

It now appeared that Sylvester had decided to live in our backyard, so I bought a little plastic storage box for him to seek shelter in when it rained. He evidenced his appreciation for this kindness showed to him by actually using it. My dad and stepmother, Norma, were visiting from Ohio in late October and they thought it rather cute how he went into his little box. Since they thought he was so cute, I decided I'd take this a step farther and bring him into the house. On this particular night, a monstrous thunderstorm was on the horizon heading our way, so that validated my desire to bring him in. He was my new little friend and I wanted him to be somewhere safe, and in with us seemed the best choice to me. He came in but didn't appear happy about it because he clawed frantically at the door and meowed to be let back out. My husband said I'd better put him back outside because he probably belonged to somebody, and I was stealing somebody's cat. That idea was absurd, but I think the main reason he said it was because Sylvester was annoying him with all the commotion he was making. We knew he didn't belong to anyone—he was just a bony, walking skeleton of a cat. Even if the remotest possibility did exist that someone owned him, they certainly didn't deserve to. No one or no thing should be starved and ignored like he was. As I recall, we did succumb to his relentless, pitiful crying and put him back outside that night and he slept in his box. Apparently the box

He became somewhat of a permanent fixture in the back yard.

was waterproof because the next morning he was dry and happy, and seemed content with his living arrangements.

He became somewhat of a permanent fixture in the back yard. After he ate he would nap all day close to the house under the pine tree. It was the same tree Nina had chosen for the location of her home, and consequently the same tree under which I buried her. I had decided to be a better person to him, and I was. I also decided that if Sylvester was to become one of us then he needed to go to the vet for some vaccinations and male surgery. In his waking hours he was fighting with each and every other cat that came his way, especially an all white stray, later to be named Snowball. I thought perhaps that this altering of him might mellow him out a bit and his combative instincts would go away. That was the main reason. I really didn't plan on making him our official third cat child or anything radical like that. Plus he just didn't have a very healthy look about him and I didn't want him spreading any diseases to our other two cats. His mouth was always hanging slightly open, as if he were having a hard time breathing, which originally was another reason he did not look very appealing to me. He needed, most importantly, a check up.

I had previously taken, on separate occasions, two other stray cats to the vet because they appeared sickly and needed medical attention. Both never returned. One had been in an accident at some point in his life and had a broken hip. It had healed leaving him somewhat of a cripple, which later caused internal problems, including loss of bladder control. As the vet put it, "He's no spring chicken and things will never get any better for him." Another seemed to have a terrible cold and runny eyes and he ended up testing positive for FIV (Feline Immunodeficiency Virus). At the veterinarian's suggestion, both of them had been put to sleep.

Sylvester seemed to have a very trusting look in his eyes when he looked at me; it was almost like he worshipped me. I made a promise to him that he would make it back from the veterinarian, no matter what the verdict was about him. I couldn't take another cat to its death when I was only trying to help it. It just didn't seem right. Plus I had become attached to my new friend in the back yard.

My strong mindset was to be challenged. He also tested positive for FIV. Feline Immunodeficiency Virus (FIV) is a chronic immunodeficiency disease in cats. It is a retrovirus, which is similar to the AIDS virus in humans. The vet suggested euthanasia would be best. She said it was not fair to the neighborhood to just neuter him and put him back out on the streets. She was right, of course. It is a contagious virus and he would spread it if he got into a fight and bit another cat. I wondered if there was a cat around he had not already been in a fight with and bitten, but I didn't mention that. I wasn't sure what I was going to do with him. The only thing I was sure about was that he was coming back home with me. After all, I had promised him. I had also promised myself that I would not take another cat to its death.

> *My strong mindset was to be challenged. He also tested positive for FIV. The vet suggested euthanasia would be best.*

Safely back home, away from the euthanasia needle, I wondered exactly what I would do with him. Since he had just had surgery, I thought it best to keep him in the basement for the night. I didn't want any of his former or present adversaries to come calling when he was still groggy from the anesthetic. He was already well acquainted with and accepted by our other two cats, so his sleeping over for a night was okay with them.

We all woke up to a white-carpeted winter wonderland the next morning. It was November so this really wasn't any surprise or shock. It had turned much colder during the night and started snowing heavily. There were several inches on the ground already. Snow was still falling in the morning and when I opened the door for Sylvester to go back outside he just looked at me. A blustery wind complete with snow blew in on his face; he turned around and headed back into the house. He gave me one of those looks that only cats can give, as if he was saying, "No, no, I'm not that kind of cat anymore. I live in here now." So that's how he ended up to be a housecat; he just decided it one day. He had been there and done the outside thing, and now he had found a better life and was smart enough to realize it. He did eventually venture back out in the daytime but came in at night with our other two cats. I would tell him to go in the peace of Jesus and pray for him so he wouldn't get into any fights. I would occasionally hear him making those loud, jarring cat noises when he was in a standoff with another cat, and I would go get him. Since I usually intervened in these pre-fight cat conversations, I hoped he wasn't fighting anymore, just thinking about it.

In the past we had spraying (of urine) problems with our other two cats, which is the reason why they were confined to the basement at night and sent outside for the day. New living room furniture had made this a permanent arrangement for them, since the previous furniture had been some of their favorite targets. Occasionally in the evening we would leave the basement door open to see what Sylvester would do. He was very curious and would come up to see what was happening with us. He particularly liked to go upstairs to the second floor. Not knowing what sort of mannerisms he would have (most importantly spraying or not spraying), we promptly followed him and suggested he go back downstairs to where we could keep an eye on him. He complied because he just liked being with us. He didn't play or get into things; he was content just to sit quietly by us or lay on the floor.

Sylvester really did not want me to tell you about this next incident, but when I explained to him that perhaps by doing so we could possibly help other cats with the same problem, he consented to its being told. Every time he joined us, we noticed an awful smell often accompanied him. We realized that he was experiencing flatulence after eating. Yes, poor Sylvester had "cat gas, " which one family member kindly termed "fluffs." So for awhile he was nicknamed Fluffy. Shortly thereafter he returned to the vet to be treated for a case of ear mites, so we mentioned this little unpleasant problem to her. She said that often cats are allergic to the artificial coloring in commercial cat foods, so she suggested a few brands with no artificial coloring. We started feeding him a different food and the problem was solved. There hasn't been a need to call him Fluffy since then and we are all very happy about that.

I had this doom and gloom attitude about him, since the vet had more or less pronounced a death sentence over him. I told my daughter not to get too attached to him because of his diagnosis, and I was also a bit leery about her handling him. I wasn't quite sure if this virus was transmittable to humans or not. Of course, it is not, as I later learned, but at the time I wasn't taking any chances with my only child. The vet had said to make his remaining days comfortable for him, and not to cause him any unnecessary stress. He would be visiting upstairs with us and when it was time for him to return to the basement for the night he would balk, repeatedly, at being put back into the basement. He would put on his brakes at the top of the steps and we would literally have to push him down and quickly shut the door. I felt awful about ejecting him out of the house and shoving him down the steps. I feared that this was a stressful situation for him and wanted to avoid it if we could. I hated it as much as he did. With this in mind, my husband and I decided to let Sylvester choose where he wanted to sleep— upstairs or downstairs. So at night when we opened the basement door, if he wanted to go down, all well and good; if he didn't then he stayed upstairs. Now enters the fact that we have a security alarm in the house with motion detectors and cannot have any little moving bodies in the house at night. So if he wanted to be upstairs, he had to sleep with us in our bedroom. Perfect. He couldn't have planned it better himself, or maybe he did. Needless to say, it has now been years since he's last slept in the basement. Can you imagine him going from an unwanted pest in the backyard to a bed buddy in about six month's time?

As my affection grew for this unlikely candidate, so did my desire to protect him. For a number of reasons, I began keeping him in the house more and more. Several new strays had appeared upon the scene, tomcats of course, and I didn't want him to be injured in any fights. He also was used to spending many hours in the park, presumably hunting mice, and this activity required him to cross the street in order to get to the park. Although our street isn't very long, cars race down it at a disturbing speed. Since we had one cat run over and were blessed to have her miraculously escape without injuries, I didn't want to take any chances with Sylvester.

An incident happened one evening that made me decide some permanent changes had to be made. When my husband and I left to go out one evening, all three of them, Windy, Augel, and Sylvester, were sitting on the front steps. We had only gone a block or two when I remembered that I had forgotten something, so we returned home to get it. All three of them were now in the park across the street. Remember that this was just minutes after we left. They were just like disobedient children, waiting for our backs to be turned to do something that they knew they were not allowed to do. Whenever I did see one of them venture into the park I would go to get them. As soon as they saw me coming across the street, they usually would run back home. Once back in our yard they would look at me with that, "Yeah, yeah, I know I wasn't supposed to be there look." So I knew that they knew they were not supposed to cross the street and go into the park. Windy and Augel definitely knew that the park was off limits and they were not being very good examples for Sylvester. Then and there the decision was made that if I could not trust them, then they would have to stay in more, especially when we were not home.

Neighborhoods change from time to time, and ours changed when, as I mentioned earlier, some thug cats moved in. It was no longer safe for Sylvester to be outside alone at all. It appeared that the desire of his heart was to be our housecat, so we granted his wish. He has some 'fresh air time' every day under my supervision in the fenced in backyard. He has to stay with me in the yard and he learned very quickly that he was not to jump over the fence. The few times he did go over the fence, I explained to him he was not to do that anymore, so he didn't. That's Sylvester, always ready to please. He's also extremely smart so he learns things very quickly. He made it his goal not only to weasel his way into our house and our lives, but also to become the perfect house pet. He succeeded.

Chapter 3

Over and Oops

Even the best cat will have a day when it's just too hard to remain perfect. One such day was a Saturday in March, which started out to be a lovely spring morning. I had taken Sylvester out earlier than usual. By his actions he had indicated to me that he liked me to wait until the afternoon to take him out—when all the dew was gone. He didn't like walking on the wet grass and getting his feet all wet. On this particular morning I became engrossed in the inspection of my spring flower bulbs. I'll admit that I wasn't monitoring him as closely as I should have been, but as I said, he had learned the yard rules and it had been quite some time since he had escaped or even attempted it. However, when I looked for him I realized he had suddenly disappeared. To my alarm he had jumped the fence! Something on the other side of the fence was too irresistible and he couldn't help himself. The subject of his intense scrutiny was Woolly Cat, a stray tomcat, with whom Sylvester had been in a pretty hateful fight a few years back. Woolly Cat, most likely needing to fight to exist, wasn't playing games, and at that time Sylvester had received several nasty bites on his neck. Sylvester, although not a fighter anymore, had a score to settle if the opportunity ever presented itself, and with only a fence separating them, it was clear to him that the opportunity had presented itself.

I had to think quickly—I couldn't go out the gate to get him because that would chase Woolly Cat in Sylvester's direction. Given their present proximity, there was only about five feet between them. My only option was to go over the fence. The fence was not quite four feet tall, but it was an unfriendly little fellow in that it had sharp wire prongs protruding at the top, which I needed to be sure to clear as I hurled myself over it. For anyone watching, I imagine this was not a very graceful maneuver on my part. I didn't land on my feet as I planned, but rather fell with a hard thud in a crumpled mess. But I had made it over and had landed between Sylvester and Woolly Cat—that was the important part. My sudden falling from the sky, which I'm sure is what it appeared like to the cats, scared Woolly so badly that he took off as fast as his little feet would go. Only after the initial problem of separating the cats was accomplished, did I realize that I had excruciating pain coming from a number of locations on my body. The worst pain was coming from my foot. At first I thought I had landed on a board with a nail in. This area was a collect all spot beside my neighbor's garage, so that was a possibility. I looked around for the offending board, but there was nothing there except grass. Then I looked at my foot. My sock and shoe were soaked with blood so something worse than just a nail must have happened to it. I scooped Sylvester up and limped into the house the best I could. Although hurting, I felt satisfied that I had accomplished my mission—I rescued him and prevented him from getting into another big fight.

My husband is rarely home on Saturday mornings because that is his golf time. Fortunately for me, this morning he had a later tee time and had stopped back home after doing some errands. At first he thought I was just acting silly by limping so badly, but then he saw my face distorted by pain and knew something was very wrong. Then, as he noticed my bright red foot, I noticed him turn ashen white—evidencing how he doesn't handle blood and injuries very well. I said I could handle this myself and he should be off to the golf course. He thought I was going to pass out probably because he felt like he was going to pass out, so he rushed me off to the doctor, being dramatically more concerned with the situation than I was. I'll avoid the gory details for the squeamish and faint of heart and just say that I needed nine stitches on the arch area of my foot and had a few other minor cuts on my arm and leg. I had to be on crutches for over a week. Apparently, I had caught my foot on one of the prongs on the top of the fence on my way over.

Sylvester never did fully realize the price I paid for his disobedience that day, but he did know that something bad had happened. I think he also knew he had played a major role in it. He would come and sit by me and look very sad, so I interpreted that as his expression of sympathy for me. I'm sure he was sorry. What more could I ask for?

Although I often wonder, I'll never know for sure where he came from. I don't know if he ever lived in a house or not, but he definitely acted like he didn't know the first thing about houses or about people when we first brought him inside. As I mentioned, he first decided the house was the better place to be when he realized that, although the temperature turned cold outside, it remained warm inside. At first, much of the activity in the house during the day frightened him. For several months the doorbell was a mystifying source of total terror for him. He would utterly freeze in his tracks, wide-eyed with fright. If someone would actually come in, he'd scramble double time up the steps and hide under our bed. He reminded me of the way movies portray backwoods people that seldom see strangers. If someone comes, you see them run inside and peek out the windows. Well, he did the same thing. If I was talking to someone outside, he'd peak around the curtain to see who it was. Obviously all the house noises such as the can opener, the vacuum cleaner, the hair dryer, and an endless array of other things were new and thus very scary to him. Another thing I noticed was that he was terrified when you picked things up. If you had something in your hand and happened to look his way, he was gone. I wondered if people had thrown things at him or if it was just that these items were unfamiliar objects to him. I tried to be considerate of his very sensitive nature and would show him things before I made noises with them, or would show him the things later that had frightened him. In time, he learned that no one who visited us would ever hurt him, and all the new sounds were harmless. He started to feel that his new home was a safe sanctuary and he began to trust us. My husband constantly commented on what tremendous progress Sylvester was making in not being so paranoid. Today noises no longer frighten him and he actually lets me vacuum him with the brush attachment to the vacuum cleaner. I guess it feels good on his back, or at least that's the impression I get. Another of his favorite devices is the electric hand-held back massager. As soon as he hears the hum of it, he is there butting you with his head to get you to do his back too. Like Rich says, he has come a long way.

Chapter 4

Grandma, the Mangia Man & Jen-No-Fur

Sylvester was just about convinced that his new home was a safe sanctuary—heaven on earth. Then it happened—my mother and stepfather, Frank, came for a visit. This was the first time they had seen him and vice-versa. They usually come either for Thanksgiving or Christmas, and this particular year it must have been for Christmas. No one had ever come and stayed before, so this was an entirely new experience for Sylvester. It got off to a really awful start as far as Sylvester was concerned. It had been snowing so my mother wanted to sweep the snow off the steps before we started carrying their suitcases and all the Christmas packages in. When she picked the broom up, I cautioned her not to make any sudden movements with it because it would frighten Sylvester. As he walked by her, she shook it at him and said, "See, this is nothing to be afraid of." Well, to him that stick coming at him definitely was something to be afraid of! He shot up the steps and stayed under the bed for the rest of the day. I had to take his supper up to him because he *would not* come back downstairs even to eat. Even now, whenever they come he spends almost the entire first day under the bed. For a reason known only to him, the broom coming at him that day long ago has stuck in his

Frank and Dorothy Gadzia & Jennafer

memory and there is no getting it out.

To add to the scenario, my stepfather has a louder, deeper voice than what Sylvester is used to hearing. The sound of it sends shock waves through the poor cat for the first few days of their visit. However, toward the end of their visit last time, Sylvester decided to become sociable and joined us for a while in the evening. Then events took a strange turn and in the end Sylvester and Frank became bosom buddies. I think this was the result of Frank's sneaking Sylvester excessively large amounts of treats. Sylvester gets two or three Pounce Tartar Control treats several times a day, and I thought that if some of the treats came from these interlopers, that Sylvester might be more inclined to take a liking to them. Frank made the comment that I was being very stingy with the treats. "After all," he said, "You have a whole bag of them." I guess he thought they were like a bag of potato chips to us, and you could just eat and eat them until you had gulped down the entire bag. You see, my stepfather is Italian, and you know how Italians like to feed you. Frank's favorite words are *"mangia, mangia"* (pronounced *mon-jah* and means "eat" in Italian). When I lived at home I would mangia and I became overweight; when Jennafer went for a visit, she would mangia and she came back home overweight; and I'm sure if they had a pet, it would mangia and it would be overweight too. Sylvester, being a stray cat, isn't into pedigrees or nationalities, and has no idea what an Italian or anybody else is—all he knows is he likes this mangia idea and he was hanging with the mangia man. We all commented on what great pals they had become. Frank would be sitting on the sofa and Sylvester would be right there beside him—and the bag of treats would be almost gone. It'll be interesting to see if Sylvester still feels it necessary to spend the first day in hiding under the bed the next time they visit, or if he'll welcome the mangia man back with open paws. I only hope that this latest incident makes a lasting favorable impression to replace the lasting unfavorable impression the broom made on the first visit.

Cats are supposed to be devoted to one person, so they say, and just tolerate all other family members. This is true in Sylvester's case. But then again, it would be hard to be glued to more than one person at one time, wouldn't it? For obvious reasons he picked me as his person. I was his first contact in the back yard, plus I was passing out free food. I'm sure in the beginning the food was what made the selection process so easy for him. The way I saw it, and obviously he did too, the other two family members really weren't viable choices for him. My daughter, Jennafer, for some reason scared him. Although she was in her late teens when he arrived, she would be a little rough and rowdy with him. You generally have to deal with that type of behavior from a smaller child, but since her cat, Augel, was of a different temperament and took to being swung around and danced with—stuff like that—she naturally wanted to treat this newcomer in the same manner. The dilemma was that Sylvester was too sophisticated for this frivolity. She had a favorite game she liked to play with him, which he did not find amusing *at all*. She would pick him up and play the game we named "rock-a-bye-baby." It involved her rocking him like a baby in her arms as she sang the nursery song:

"Rock a bye baby in the tree top,
When the wind blows the cradle will rock.
When the bough breaks the cradle will fall,
And down will come baby, cradle and all."

The *"down will come baby"* part was her cue to let him free fall for a couple feet and then catch him. After unwillingly playing the game a few times he learned to identify the words *"rock a bye baby"* and whenever she asked him if he wanted to play *"rock a bye baby"* he would swat at her when she came to get him. He had blade sharp claws, so he set her straight about her torturous game—it was *not* for him! He called her Jen-No-Fur instead of Jennafer *(well, I'm sure he would have if he could talk)*, because her name was *Jen* and she had *"no fur"* like he did. Be assured he kept a very watchful eye on *Jen-No-Fur's* every action when she was in the vicinity.

Our third family member, my husband, spent long days at work and really had no extra time to spend with a stray cat. I was not only the logical choice for Sylvester's affection, I was the only choice.

Chapter 5
Perfect Is As Perfect Does

In many ways Sylvester became the very best cat that I ever owned. I have always described my daughter as a near perfect child, the one you would order out of a catalog if you could have your pick. I would have to describe Sylvester the same way. My friend Nora said he's so perfect that it's scary. Nora and her husband, Frank, recently took in a stay cat, and Sylvester and I would like to think that he had a small part in their decision to do so by showing them what enchanting pets cats can be. They truly can be, especially when they have temperaments like Sylvester's. He's always perfectly polite and well mannered; he displays his perfect manners in such ways as always (most always) coming when called; he never jumps onto the counters, the table, or anywhere for that matter where he is not supposed to be; and he never uses any of the furniture for a scratching post. Plus he never meows loudly or demands food. Actually most of the time he just opens his mouth and a small squeak or no sound at all comes out. I read somewhere that is how a cat asks for something very politely—by silently meowing or by making a very low-key chirrup noise. I can believe that presumption, because Sylvester is very polite. It's as if he's read and memorized the handbook on how to be the perfect housecat. But the thing I appreciate most about him is the way that he seems to thank me a hundred times a day for saving him from what would probably have been a slow death at the hands of nature, and giving him a home. He comes and sits quietly beside me and just stares mesmerized at me like I'm a goddess and he is doing homage to me. His eyes are endless pools of love and devotion. Strange how originally those same eyes were one of the reasons why I did not like him. I'll bet there are lots of people out there that we think we don't like for whatever reason, and they could become some of our best and most loyal friends if given half the chance.

Aside from the fence incident, he is 99.9% perfect 99.9% of the time except for one twofold character flaw. He's a very selfish and jealous cat when it comes to interacting with others of his species. This little problem doesn't really affect me personally, because to me he is affectionate and lovable. But the way he treats other cats, well . . . let's just say he needs a lot of improvement in that area. When our other cat Windy is visiting in the evening from the basement, he gets all his toys and lies on top of them so she cannot play with them. If she does happen to find one he missed, he goes and snatches it out from under her. They are *his* toys and he is not sharing. That goes for his food too. If another cat starts eating out of his dish, he'll reach his paw to the edge of the dish and pull it right out from under its nose. With one swift paw motion he just slides it over to him and sits there with *his* dish. He may not want to eat it, but he doesn't want anyone else eating it either. After all, it is his food. If we give another cat too much attention, he'll go upstairs to the bedroom and sulk. I've noticed recently that as the years go by, he's getting worse with his selfishness and jealousy instead of better. In his mind he definitely would like our household to be a one cat house, and of course, he'd be the one cat.

It's been many years ago, but I do remember praying for a dog to come into our yard if God thought I should have another dog. God, as always, knew what I really needed. My husband's job frequently requires him to work sixteen to twenty hour days, and the year after Sylvester came to live with us my daughter went out of state to college. I would have been very lonely without my new little buddy. He's more than a cat to me. He's my constant companion, and my very loyal friend. He really does seem to be the dog I prayed for disguised in a cat suit. Once when my husband's daughter Wendy was visiting us, she was feeling around his neck and looking at him with great curiosity. She said she was looking for a zipper because he had to be a dog in a cat costume. He acts more like a dog than any cat I ever owned. He follows me everywhere I go. Together we go upstairs, downstairs, to the basement, back and forth, and round and round the house everyday. One of his favorite things to help me do is the laundry. I'll sort the clothes into neat piles and he'll lie down on them—usually on the clothes that I need at that moment to put in the washer. So I have to move him and he settles in on another pile until I need it. Or else he'll sit there very alert, like he's the supervisor and needs to pay very close attention to exactly what I'm doing.

His other very favorite hour of entertainment is in the morning when I put my makeup on. He sits on the counter by the sink concentrating on me as I concentrate on my image in the mirror. About every five minutes he butts me with his head or rearranges my assortment of makeup items, which is his way of telling me he needs some attention. I've learned to allow additional time for this ritual. Since I'm usually getting ready to go to work or out, I feel he needs some extra time at this point because he'll be alone for several hours when I leave. I could never be mean to him or push him out of the way. He was ignored and pushed aside too much before he came to live with us. He's developed a very sensitive nature now and I want to nurture that in him. I think it is important to have sensitivity and compassion towards others, be they animals or humans.

During this time, he also developed a great fascination with water. When I'd be washing my face, he'd have his face in the sink too. Then he'd try to drink the warm water, and I, of course, would intercept him. I didn't think dirty, soapy water would be good for him. However, I noticed if I left clean, warm water in the sink he'd spend an unusually long time drinking it, lapping it slowly and leisurely like he was really savoring it. So thus began a ritual of his own—he gets warm water in the sink every morning after his breakfast and every night before bed. To add to his enjoyment, he attacks the bubbles that form in the sink as the faucet runs. He never tires of this silly game. In the end his face is all wet and he seems to be a bit annoyed by that. But then he drinks his warm water and it has its wondrous soothing effect on him, and all is well again. At this point, since he already has a good start with his face all wet, he continues washing up. He'll spend forty-five minutes cleaning himself, but that's what bathrooms are for, aren't they?

Chapter 6

God is Able!

I try to start off each day with time spent reading my Bible and in prayer. Sylvester for some reason likes that time, because he almost always comes to sit by me as soon as I open my Bible. One day he appeared intently interested in it all, so I actually found myself explaining to him what a Bible is and all about God and how Jesus died for our sins and someday we will live in heaven with Him. Sometimes I even read the Bible out loud to him. So everyday he became my little buddy at prayer time. I would ask God to bless him and make him healthy. I believe God honored those simple prayers prayed for a cat because Sylvester never ever manifested any symptoms of FIV. One year after his original visit, I took him to the vet for his check-up and she was surprised to see how well he was doing. I told her I believed God had healed him and he no longer had FIV. She looked at me like I had just grown a second head. No matter, Sylvester and I know what we believe. The Bible says whatsoever things you want when you pray, believe that you'll receive them and you'll have them. In our natural thinking we want to pray and receive, and once we see it or receive it, then we'll believe. My understanding is that that's not the order God wants us to operate in.

It's now been six years since Sylvester came into our back yard and into our lives, and he's still perfectly healthy. You may be wondering, does God really care enough about a cat to heal him? Personally, I have no doubt God does care and that Sylvester's health is no coincidence. God created animals, hence I'm convinced He cares about them. But more importantly, God cares about us, his children. He'll answer our prayers, as we believe in faith, whether they are prayers for small, seemingly unimportant matters or prayers for big, life threatening situations.

Moreover, statistics prove that pets keep us healthy, they lessen stress in our lives, and they provide companionship for us. That in itself would be reason enough to keep our pets around. When they are happy and healthy, we are happy and healthy. I believe Sylvester is healed and I am thankful to the Lord for doing it. I give God the glory, and whenever I can I tell Sylvester's story of healing to encourage other people. My prayer is that his story will inspire you to believe in God for things you thought impossible—whether they are miniscule or grandiose. God is able!

End

Ode to Sylvester

Pink nose and yellow eyes, didn't look quite right to me,
But he showed me things that on my own I couldn't see

Often we have needs another human can't meet,
But the answer walks into our lives on four feet.

Sylvester, sent from above,
Not just a cat, but a gift of love.

Sylvester

Snowball's Story
From Wild to Mild

Occasionally when I looked out the kitchen window I would see something white slinking through the neighbor's back yard. Or late at night before I'd go to bed, I would gaze from my bedroom window into the park and see a lone white figure disappearing in the tree shadows. Or did I?

I gave a name to everything that moved in my life. My car's name was Thunder—this being derived from the fact that the color stated on the invoice was thunder black. A baby opossum that showed up in our back yard was named Opie. When a friend accompanied aptly dubbed was only white animal named. I Snowball.

He was obviously a wild stray cat, very afraid of humans, avoiding even the remotest contact with them at all costs.

of Opie's him, he was Scopey. So it logical this also be named him Snowball the cat. I know this was not a very original name for a white cat, but as I recall, I gave him this name more as an identifying factor than for any other reason.

He was obviously a wild stray cat, very afraid of humans, avoiding even the remotest contact with them at all costs. On numerous occasions I made fruitless attempts to coax him into the yard with food. This white cat fascinated me; I had never personally known a white cat. Although for almost all my life since childhood I had a cat of some sort, I never had a white one. White cats, to me, were supposed to be pampered house pets, pristine white, groomed immaculately, and probably wearing a rhinestone collar. They were not supposed to belong to no one; they were not supposed to be a stray nobody roaming my neighborhood. My goal became to get to know him. I bought what seemed to be some very appealing canned cat food, the kind whose smell was so potent that it lingered for hours in the house after you opened the can. Here was my plan. The next time I spotted him I would run and get the food, race outside, get his attention, and leave the food on a paper plate. I knew his keen sense of smell would surely pick up on this scrumptious meal awaiting him. It worked, and so began the process of getting to know Snowball. He began to associate my presence with a very tasty dining experience. Soon I could actually stand a distance away while he ate. This continued for two years. Eventually, he permitted me to sit beside him, but not too close; he still preferred a little distance between us. Any sudden movement or noise sent him dashing off, and most of the time he didn't return even to finish his meal.

Then one day I did the unthinkable. He had finally allowed me to sit right beside him and converse with him while he ate. All of a sudden, as he was deeply engrossed in eating, I reached out and petted his little head. As I started scratching his ears he closed his eyes, stopped eating, and sat up like he was lost in a world of ecstasy. He appeared to love the idea of someone scratching his head! Then he opened his eyes and actually saw what was happening—a human was touching him! His eyes became huge with an expression of shock and fright and he darted off. Even so, it was truly the event of the summer. I called my husband, Rich, at work and told him the astonishing news. He was just as surprised as I was and wanted to know all the details of how it happened. Even my good friends on our street, who were familiar with his situation, were surprised to learn that finally someone had touched him. It was a while before I tried it again, but eventually he did accept a few pets here and there. Then my husband got involved in this story and Snowball also accepted him as someone who he'd permit to pet him. The fact my husband was the "breakfast man" at 5:30 a.m. probably accounted for this endearing fondness the cat had for him.

Once again, one day I did the unthinkable. I reached right down and picked him up! Just like that. I held him, scratched his ears for a moment, and put him back down. He wasn't so shocked this time; he just had a confused expression on his face. He seemed to ask, "What was the purpose of that?" There did end up being a very valuable purpose for it. In the third year of our acquaintance I picked him up and quickly placed him into a cat carrier and drove him to the vet for a checkup, shots, and a future appointment for neutering. He was very healthy and about four years old. I also learned from the vet what the black spot on his pink nose was. He had a perfectly pink little nose with this black spot on the corner. I was never able to get a close enough look at it to figure out what it was. The vet said it was just black pigment. He had a pink nose with a black spot on it, plain and simple. More importantly, I learned to my surprise he was already neutered. Don't ask me how I missed that one. He did have a lot of hair being an outside cat in the winter and all. Some parts of him remained fuzzier than others, even in the summer; that's my defense. About this same time my neighbor Frank told me that Snowball looked to be expecting— when did I think the kittens would arrive? He thought

> *Life was good for Snowball. He spent most of his time on our front steps or under the bushes in the front of the house.*

perhaps that he and his wife, Nora, would adopt one. So he thought Snowball was a she! I felt good knowing more people than just I were confused about the gender of this cat. Apparently, since he was neutered, he did have a home at some point in his life, and for whatever reason had become a stray cat without a home when I befriended him. This poor homeless creature acted like he had been severely abused in his early years of life. Surely something had to have happened to him to cause him to be so totally paranoid of humans by the time he showed up in our neighborhood.

Life was good for Snowball. He got two meals a day; breakfast and supper, like clockwork. Even when we lost daylight savings time in the fall, he still got his supper on time—his time. We kept the cats on a regular schedule, so our 5:30 p.m. was really their 4:30 p.m. We tried not to confuse them but I think we confused ourselves more in the process. His good life included a few other cat friends in the neighborhood, plus he had our cat Windy to hang out with in the daytime. She, being a little girl cat, had to come in the house at night. I am a firm believer that girls should not be out all night, animals or human. He spent most of his time on our steps or under the bushes in the front of the house. He was a real homebody. He was always there when we came home from anywhere. My husband started this nightly treat thing with him. Sometime between 9:00 and 10:00 p.m. or whenever we got home if we were out, Snowball would get a bedtime snack. His snack was the soft cat food in the little packets. At this point in his life he had graduated from the smelly canned food to hard food, the premium high quality kind bought in pet stores, so this nightly tasty treat was greatly anticipated. That was pretty much the routine for him and for us. He was always there. Sometimes he would let you pet him and sometimes he ran away. Day in and day out, it was the same with him. A very strange cat. Actually we wondered at times whether he had a mental imbalance, his behavior was that bizarre. We were nothing but nice to him, so how come he would run from us half of the time? It sure seemed like he had been hit on the head or had an accident at some prior point in his life which created this mental imbalance. We gladly accepted whatever he accepted. We didn't push him to be our best cat friend or anything like that. It was just nice to have him around. He was always there.

At this time we had three other cats: Sylvester, Augel, and Windy. Sylvester was a housecat, Windy went outside in the daytime (weather permitting), and Augel stayed in the basement and accompanied my daughter to her room when she came home. Each floor of our house usually had a cat in residence. We really didn't need another cat in the house, but we did offer this option to Snowball. He refused. One very cold night I brought him into the basement and he **YOWLED!!** all night. Snowball didn't have a normal meow like a normal cat. He **YOWLED!!** A yowl is a very loud, top of the lungs meow. Not a living creature in our household slept that night. He made his point loud and clear that even in the cold of winter, he preferred to be outside. Of course, we didn't allow him to be totally on his own out there in the freezing cold and snow. We constructed a little house for him out of a plastic storage container. It had a mouse-type hole cut for a door with clear plastic over it to keep the wind out. He would use his little paw to open the door and go into his house. Once inside he lounged on an old rug topped with a piece of a bed comforter (very soft and cushy) and on top of that a thermal animal pad with a towel on it. All in all, it seemed to keep him quite warm and he would spend most of his time in the winter in his house. We located it in our backyard where we could view it from our dining room window—just to keep an eye on him. He loved his little house. This was one thing we did that he seemed to totally approve of. In his opinion we were good house builders.

His wacko personality was a little hard to take sometimes because he did appear to be such a cute cat. Sometimes you would just want to touch him or pick him up and give him a hug, but you could never count on that with Snowball. He needed a big investment of time to bring him around and the time just never seemed available, so we left well enough alone. When I wanted an affectionate cat, I would go to Sylvester to meet my emotional need. However, for some unknown reason, he wanted my husband to pick him up and hold him briefly before he would start eating his breakfast. His morning hug was more important to him than food. Then often in the afternoon you couldn't get near him. He truly was a very peculiar cat.

Chapter 2

Missing!

February 21, 1998 was a rather normal Saturday. Thus far we had had an unusually warm winter with only one snowfall recorded, presumably due to El Nino. The spring-like weather made you want to start doing yard work and other outside chores. I went outside around noon and Snowball was sitting by the side door looking for lunch. Yes, I forgot to mention that life was now very good for Snowball and he was getting three meals a day. My schedule permitted me to be home around the noon hour and since I ate lunch I thought lunch was in order for the cats. When my husband found they were also getting "lunch," he suggested that perhaps I should think about doing away with this meal. My part time work hours could be changing soon and I wouldn't be home at noon any longer. Today seemed like as good a day as any to start the new "no lunch" schedule, so the cats did not have lunch. We had plans to go to my sister-in-law's for dinner, so I decided to give the cats their supper a little early—only fifteen minutes early. Fifteen minutes is not a big time difference, but then again maybe it is to a cat. Snowball was not there so I left his food outside near the side door in a little, very expensive doghouse we had bought for him. Originally this little doghouse was supposed to be his home, but he didn't like it. He wasn't into materialism and appearances for the sake of other cats, so he preferred his $5.99 storage container to an expensive home. Since it was such a costly little investment, it remained outside the door and became the Cat's Restaurant, as my friend Nora called it. I had last seen him snoozing in the backyard at 2:30 p.m., so I assumed that when he woke up he had gone for one of his walks. When he did venture out of our yard, which really wasn't very often, he would go down the block a few houses and usually be gone for an hour or so. I didn't panic because he wasn't there.

We returned home that night close to midnight and checked the Cat Restaurant to see if he had eaten his food. His food hadn't been touched. This was quite unusual because Snowball was not one to miss a meal. Also, it was past time for his bedtime snack so he should have been waiting for us as soon as we pulled into the driveway. Now I was concerned. I wanted to walk around the block to look for him, but Rich thought it not a great idea at midnight. He said Snowball would be back in the morning for his breakfast. He wasn't. This was not like Snowball. He had always been there. Sometimes Windy would be missing for half a day or so and we'd find her in the garage. She was the curious sort that couldn't pass up investigating an opened door. Since yesterday was such a nice day, many people could have been in their garages doing work and using gardening tools and he could have wandered in. Before I left for church I looked in our garage. Then I made a few quick calls to our neighbors and asked them to also check in their garages. He was no where to be found.

I pray about everything in my life and have a pretty good average of about eighty percent answered favorably. So Sunday morning in church I confidently prayed for the return of Snowball, and expected him to be sitting on the front steps when I came home. He wasn't. I immediately changed my clothes and walked the entire neighborhood in search of him. The weather had changed drastically from yesterday, becoming quite cold. As I endlessly searched, my hands became like ice cubes and I found myself shivering. I wondered if Snowball was cold and shivering wherever he was. I had to find him. As I walked past the houses I glanced at all the windows in the event someone had taken him in, unaware that he already belonged to someone. I know cats like to sit in windows and look out, so I couldn't help myself—my eyes focused on each and every window in hopes I would see his little white face with the pink nose with the black spot on it looking out. I didn't and in reality wasn't surprised. Remembering his paranoid nature, I decided it would be highly unlikely that he would permit someone else to take him in. When I returned home I made a few phone calls to people in the neighborhood who knew him. No one had seen him for days.

I thought maybe it was mating season for cats and he got all caught up in the excitement of it even though he was neutered. An animal shelter later told me that type thing does not happen. They probably thought me some kind of idiot for even asking if it was possible. The reason I wondered about it is because *all* the cats in the neighborhood were missing. There had been several strays that were regulars at the restaurant. Among the regulars were a little black cat, a mousy gray cat, a longhaired tiger cat, a very nervous little cat that looked exactly like Windy, and two cats owned by neighbors. They would check what was on the menu for the day and then hang out in the backyard for awhile. It became very mysterious when not a single cat was visible in the entire neighborhood. They all had to be somewhere doing something. I joked about how they must all be away for a weekend cat convention somewhere. I kept thinking up silly stuff like that to not dwell on all the unpleasant possibilities.

I tried to think of everything, and remembered that on Saturday there had been people canvassing our neighborhood in the morning. They were asking if anyone in the household spoke Spanish. I recall four of them standing in front of our house, talking and pointing to Snowball while he slept in the bushes. At the time I thought they were just admiring his cuteness and I really didn't think any more about it. Then afterwards I started to wonder if they had kidnapped him. This, however, was in the morning and I did see him at 2:30 p.m., so I dispelled that idea. As I said, it would be very hard for someone to capture him. It's strange all the stuff that goes through your mind.

He didn't show up for his supper and the sun set on Sunday. It was now officially twenty-four hours that he had been missing. Had he been human, I could have filed a missing person report and got the police involved. However, his being just a cat, it was up to me to find him. But for you cat owners and lovers, you know there is no such thing as *just a cat*. They may be only cats to some people, but they are little people to us, and my little furry person was missing.

I was teaching a computer class at a local college, and this particular week my class was cancelled due to lack of enrollment for the current subject. This extra time worked out well. All previous plans were set aside. First thing Monday morning I walked the entire neighborhood again to no avail. Since we live across the street from a park, I thought I'd better search through it also. I realized that this would not be a pleasant stroll through the park because if I found him there he wouldn't be alive. Despite posted leash laws, too many people were allowing their dogs to run free. Additionally, almost every person that got a dog in the last six months purchased a Rottweiler (they are the big, black, massive dogs that have become so popular). If Snowball had been taking a hike through the park and met up with one of them, I don't think he would have come out on the winning side. If someone's dog had killed him they probably would have thrown him into the weeds by the bank of the stream that ran through the park. This morbid search only took about half an hour and fortunately produced no results. Well, at least I knew and was thankful for one thing that had not happened to him. I really didn't know where else to look so I went home and busied myself with creating a missing cat poster on my computer to circulate throughout the neighborhood. At the bottom I asked everyone to please check inside their garages, sheds, and any outside storage areas in case he did wander in and became trapped. I didn't want to waste time by going to the print shop, so I ran off fifty copies using my printer and was ready to go with them in about half an hour.

I needed a friend and some moral support, so I called my friend Nora. Even though it had started raining, it didn't phase us as we set about stapling the posters on all the corner telephone poles. Then we went door to door with them until the rain became so heavy that we had to stop. Once inside the house, however, I decided I couldn't stop just yet. Time was critical if he were trapped somewhere. I printed more posters and I went back out into the pouring rain alone. I didn't quit until the one hundredth poster was tacked up and my folder was empty. Each and every house on each and every surrounding street was now aware that my cat was missing. Whether they wanted to know or not, they knew. You would have had to be blind not to know. It was very painful for me to ride down our street and to see all the posters, or to stand on the porch and look off in the distance and see them across the park. The fact my Snowball was missing was reinforced everywhere I looked.

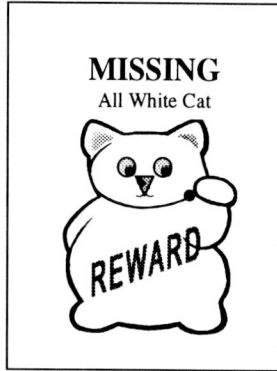

MISSING
All White Cat
REWARD

That evening a friend named Sandy who lives at the end of our street called in response to the flyer he received. I considered this an unusually kind gesture on his part, because Snowball was not one of his favorite creatures. Sandy avidly appreciated fine cars and owned several of them. Snowball showed his appreciation for the fine cars by spraying their highly polished chrome wheels. After we adopted Snowball he didn't go all the way to the end of the street very often, which Sandy appreciated. Sandy called because he happened to be up after midnight on Saturday evening and saw Snowball going through the park at a pretty good pace heading for the main street. He said he definitely looked like a cat on a mission, with someplace to go. This was very strange. Wouldn't Snowball at least eat his supper before heading off on an adventure? I wondered if something had not snapped in his head and he had become completely disoriented. Or perhaps he remembered he previously had a home somewhere else and he was heading back to his original owner. As I mentioned, we had questioned if he had a mental imbalance, so this would have been a more realistic reasoning than thinking someone had kidnapped him. In view of this new information, I expanded my search in the direction he was last presumed to be headed. More posters were made and posted. Sandy also suggested putting posters in front of the local candy and newspaper store, which was a couple blocks away. All the kids hung out there after school and kids always know where to find missing stuff.

Also on Monday two other people called saying be sure to check at the animal shelter. I was elated that my posters were generating so many calls. The first caller related the story how her cat had been picked up and taken to the shelter. She had to go bail him out. The other caller reported that their neighbor's cat was found there also. A trip to the animal shelter was definitely put at the top of the list. All the other cats in the neighborhood were still missing, so I decided to take two cat carriers to the pound just in case there had been a major cat-roundup. Of all the strays, "Woolly Cat" (the longhaired tiger cat) was my favorite, so if he were there he would be coming back home too.

Our local animal shelter was closed on Monday so we had to wait until the next day. My husband and I were there promptly at 9:00 a.m. only to find out that it didn't open until noon. What a long morning that was. To pass the time we went to the next town's shelter to check it out. They did have a few white cats from other localities and one longhaired white cat, but none from our area. The situation became grimmer and sadder, realizing so many animals were out there either lost or without homes. Finally the noon hour arrived and we were back at the animal shelter. My husband waited in the car, giving me strict instructions not to return with a dog. I had never mentioned anything about replacing our dog that had died eight years ago, so where that assumption came from I'll never know. Maybe he thought I was so mentally distraught I would do something like that.

Once inside, it seemed as if the two employees at the pound were misplaced policemen playing good cop/ bad cop. As soon as I walked in one demanded rather gruffly to know what I wanted. I had one of my posters and explained that my cat was missing, my all white cat was missing. He indifferently ordered to me to put my name, address, and phone number in the upper right corner of it (although all this information was already on it) and said someone would put it on the bulletin board. I obeyed. He vanished from the room. A very sweet lady, who called me honey, said it was too bad this was not last week because they had several white cats last week. Not much help to me since my cat wasn't missing last week. I didn't want to know where they were this week. The man then came back and said, "Follow me." We went past a row of cages that turned and made an L-shape. The very last cage contained a white cat. I got so excited. I knew we'd find him! He was all scrunched in the cage with his head down. I told the man I had to see his nose to see if it was pink with a black spot on it. He looked at me like I was crazy and said, "I'd think if it was your cat that he'd be happy to see you," and walked away. Not necessarily. You never knew if Snowball would be happy to see you or not. Then the nice lady came over and opened the cage and picked the cat up. It wasn't Snowball. This cat had an all pink nose. Snowball had put on some weight, but this was a very large, fat cat. Your mind can play tricks on you and I think I knew it wasn't him the minute I saw this cat—but I really wanted it to be him. My hopes were riding sky high when the man indicated they had a white cat, and then they came crashing down. It was almost unbearable. I was very encouraged about finding him here since two cats in my neighborhood had ended up at this shelter, but it was not to be. On my way out I checked inside all the cages, trying hard not to make eye contact with the poor unfortunates inside. I was looking for Woolly Cat; but he wasn't there either.

Tears welled up in my eyes as I returned to the car. Poor Rich thought I was crying because they had put Snowball to sleep. You hear stories sometimes that animals have only so many days to be claimed and then they become victims of euthanasia. The situation was even sadder because there was a white cat there. What was going to happen to it? I was sad for it; I was sad for me. I thought of adopting it, but we really didn't need, or even want another cat. What I wanted was my cat back and what I needed now was just to be very, very sad for awhile. Feelings of sadness turned into feelings of hopelessness. It was a hard feeling to shake. We rode home in silence.

The next call came the following day. A lady had a white cat with a black tail and a black spot on its head in her house. She had noticed my poster on the pole at the end of her street. Then she saw this cat, so she promptly snatched him up and took him in. (Snowball would never allow anyone to snatch him up.) Although the poster did specify an all white cat with a pink nose, she thought that I might want this one anyhow. I declined and felt bad for this guy too because he was being put back out on the street. She said he was very thin and obviously a stray cat, but she already had a cat and had to get him out of the house before her husband came home. This particular cat would be making the rounds of the neighborhood and I would get several calls about him.

On Thursday I made $100 REWARD stickers and retraced my steps, attaching them to all the posters on the poles. The elementary school was only two streets away so I increased the coverage around it. Kids can become extraordinary detectives when money is involved, or so I hoped. It worked. Approximately forty-five minutes after school was let out my phone rang. A little boy called to say my cat was in his backyard. He gave me his address and I realized he lived on the next street, only about ten houses away. I excitedly told Sylvester I was going to get Snowball. Sylvester had been very diligent about looking out the windows with me for Snowy. Maybe he didn't understand totally, but he knew something was up with Snowball. He recognized the name and stared intensely out the window when I told him to look for Snowball. I grabbed a bag of treats and headed out. When I got there it was the white cat with the black tail again! They had put a bowl of food out for him and he was wolfing it down. He was beginning to enjoy this missing cat thing. He was getting lots of attention from many different people and good meals besides. Again I was so disappointed. The poster clearly said ALL WHITE CAT, but I could understand a little boy wanting a $100 reward. He was disappointed too. I walked home feeling helpless and wondering how much more of this I could take. I could never imagine having a child missing and going through this. I decided to be sure to pray for the people when I hear of incidents on the news from now on. I was still praying God would bring Snowball home, and watch over him wherever he currently was. That's one thing I did know. God knew where he was. I had confidence at some point He'd let me know too.

An entire week went by with just a few calls from concerned people wondering if I had found my cat yet. The two cats that belonged to people in my neighborhood had reappeared. Where they had been I don't know, but no other cats were around. Part of the reason could have been because the Cat Restaurant went out of business. What was the purpose when its favorite customer no longer frequented it?

It had now been ten days that Snowball was missing. I was also teaching an adult continuing education class at the local high school two nights a week. This particular night, Tuesday, March 3, was one of them. The phone rang fifteen minutes before I needed to leave. It was a gentleman from a few streets over in the other direction. He was just relating the message that his son had seen a white cat but that's all he knew. Then he put his wife on the phone with a few more details. The cat was sitting on their steps and when they went out it headed across the street and disappeared into the neighbor's back yard. Before it went any farther away they decided to call me. Again this was only a couple of streets away so I jumped in my car and was in front of their house within minutes. I now had only thirteen minutes to find my cat, drive back home, get dressed, and head to class. I parked the car and scoured the backyards with the boy and his mother. They were very nice and concerned, but our efforts produced no cat. I had to go. I told them to call if they spotted him. I never heard from them again. Rich and I made several trips back to that neighborhood, both on foot and in the car, but the white cat was never spotted again.

Chapter 3

The Imposter Cat

L ife went on and I did have places to go every day, but I was always looking for a white cat. Whenever I got close to home I started looking up every driveway and in every yard for Snowball. It had been twelve days and the phone had stopped ringing. Twelve days is a long time. Maybe it's all relative, but to me the last twelve days had been a *very* long time. I had a vacation planned to go to Florida, so I needed to forget about Snowball. I felt I had really done all I could do. I had walked the neighborhood over and over, I had driven all around looking for him, and I had placed posters everywhere—I didn't know what else to do. I was resigned to the fact that he was gone and it would remain a mystery as to what had happened to him.

I was to be in Florida for eight days. Although outwardly I had given up hope of ever seeing Snowball again, I was still praying for him to return, and even put in a prayer request at a church that I attended in Florida. One night my husband phoned to say he had received a call from someone who thought they had spotted him. He had followed up on the tip and was continuing to drive around looking for him, but saw nothing. A few days after I came home, we took all the posters down. I didn't want his little face to be on the telephone poles months later with all the political hopefuls and expired garage sale signs. The posters had been up for three weeks, so he obviously was not in the area. The next time Rich asked me if I wanted to go for a drive to look for Snowball, I said no. I couldn't go on doing this. It all had to end sometime. Had I kept that mindset, I believe I would have never seen him again. But something was to change.

The following Sunday in church my pastor had an excellent message on faith: How our faith can bring answers to our prayers if we don't waver. We can't think one way one day and then another way the next day. We have to remain steadfast. Also how there is power in our words. In Romans it says we can call those things which do not exist as though they do exist. It stirred something up within me. Since coming back from Florida, I had almost totally given up on ever seeing Snowball again. He was gone, vanished, and that was that. But a still small voice started saying that I have to keep the faith. In reality, I didn't know if I wanted to keep the faith. Looking all over creation for Snowball had worn me out both physically and mentally. I had previously submitted a prayer card asking our prayer group at church to pray for Snowball to come home or to be found. On my way out the door Sunday morning, Pastor John asked about the cat. I said, "No cat yet." He said, "He'll be back." I found myself agreeing with him. Sunday night I called Snowy for supper and waited in the backyard awhile. I decided if I was going to start believing for him to return that I had better start acting like it. I stood there awhile expecting to see him. I would like this to be the end of the story and to say that he appeared out of nowhere, but he didn't.

I was getting ready for work the following Tuesday morning. At approximately 7:15 I heard loud meowing at our side door. It was the side door where the restaurant was and where Snowy was always fed. I went downstairs to see who was making all the noise. When I looked out the window I was astonished to see a very dirty and extremely thin all white cat. I called Rich and said, "Snowball is back!" He came to look and then went (ran) to get him some food. We both charged outside to see him but he took off running through the back yard. He stopped a distance away, looked back at us, and then continued over the fence and out of sight. My husband commented how it didn't look like Snowy to him. He said that this cat appeared to be much bigger than Snowball and wondered why he would run from us if it was him. I argued that it was him and said he must be even more afraid now. Who knows what he went through the past few weeks? I had to leave for work so we left food out in the restaurant. As I drove to the college I had a nagging, sinking feeling. For that brief moment when he paused to look at us, his eyes may have been focused on our eyes, but my eyes were focused on his nose. No black spot. But then again, maybe the spot wasn't pigment and it was something else on his nose that finally cleared up. The vet could have been wrong. I never actually looked at the black spot that closely. That's what I told myself. It must have been some sort of wound that finally healed and now his nose was all pink.

One of Snowball's favorite places to sleep was in the front yard under a golden cypress bush. I had planted three of them in front of the house, with an assortment of other trees and bushes, and it made a nice little forest area where he liked to hang out. He felt secluded yet could see everything that was happening in the yard and in the park, plus everything occurring on the sidewalk and street. After work as I walked through the yard I caught a glimpse of something white that was almost totally hidden under one of the cypress bushes. I stopped in my tracks because not enough of the white was visible to distinguish what it was. I had to lean over before I saw two eyes on a white cat face staring back at me. I said,

"Snowy?" Like a flash he took off up the driveway. He stopped by the garage. I didn't want to frighten him completely off our property so I went into the house to get some canned cat food. I put the food by the garage, knowing he would smell it. Immediately he dove in gulping it down, but ran when I came close. I went back into the house and got the binoculars. I stared long and hard at him and still couldn't come to a decision as to whether it was Snowball or not. Rich was right. He did look a little taller, by at least an inch or so. He finished the food and headed into the back yard. As he turned to walk away from the plate; I could plainly see this was not Snowball. I felt my heart melt as if it turned to water. This cat was a tomcat. Snowball was a neutered male. That settled it. Later he curled up in the backyard in one of the spots where Snowball slept, and he also slept. I wondered why he would choose all the same spots to sleep in. It was heart wrenching to see him where my cat was supposed to be. Someone had suggested that the ground still probably had cat scent remaining. I guess he thought if they were good enough sleeping spots for somebody else they would be good enough for him. As he slept, I again got the binoculars. He was no doubt dirty, but I discovered by closer observation that the grungy discolored spot on his head was actually gray hair mixed in with the white. The same thing was also true for part of his tail. He had fooled some other people too because I had three messages on my answer machine from people who thought they had spotted my missing cat. I returned their calls, thanking them for calling but telling them that we had a stranger in our midst, not my cat.

I was still working this faith struggle through. I pondered and meditated long and hard on the *"faith is the substance of things hoped for, the evidence of things not seen"* scripture. I determined that I needed to find some substance and evidence for this whole situation. I started telling people he would be back. So what if it was now about three and a half weeks? I started saying the longer he is gone the bigger miracle it will be when he comes home. Suddenly and daily my faith was growing. My faith isn't better than anybody else's, just better than mine had been. I wasn't worried. Even if it became six months, I believed he would still be back. You hear stories like that all the time. I remembered when I was a little girl my mother would pick me up at the elementary school everyday for lunch. One day I asked her why she had brought my cat, Bootsy, and what was he doing on the sidewalk? She said she didn't bring Bootsy. We surmised he had ridden to the school underneath the car somehow. Once the car stopped he jumped down and there he was. As I recall, he preferred the ride back home *inside* the car much better. The same thing had happened to me several years ago. There was a black and white cat in our neighborhood with a very distinct white zigzag mark on his forehead—it looked like a lightning bolt. One morning when I stopped my car at work I saw him jump out from underneath it. I made an unfruitful attempt to catch him, but he was so frightened that he just took off running and was instantly out of sight. I felt very bad about it because I had driven him about six miles from home. Remarkably, he was back in about a month's time. I thought that perhaps the same sort of thing might have happened to Snowball. Living across from a park, there are always cars coming and going.

No matter what had happened to him, he'd be back one of these days. I had faith. My husband kept saying God was too busy to be concerned about a missing cat. Rich said there are starving people and wars and important stuff like that for God to deal with. We have a few theological differences, this being one of them. I reasoned if God knows each and every time a sparrow falls and even had that verse included in the Bible to show us that He cares about everything, than nothing is too small or insignificant for Him to become involved in.

I needed some substance to my faith so I began to picture Snowball back. He used to lie on the picnic table, so every time I looked at the picnic table, I saw him back on it through the *eye of faith*. I saw him back in the restaurant eating. I have a picture of him in it and I would look at it and say, "Yep, he'll be in there again." I imagined him in his house sleeping. I looked at the empty plastic storage container, but to me it was his house and he was back in it. Rich wanted to put his house out for the garbage men because one morning he saw a huge opossum come out of it. He didn't want opossums moving in and taking over our backyard. I asked him not throw it away because I said Snowball would be back and he really liked his little house. I knew I'd see him in his house again. This became a real struggle because Rich kept saying we'd never see him again—he was probably dead. He said, "He's long gone" and I said, "He won't be gone long." Rich said, "It's hopeless" and I said, "There's hope", and so it went. Every time we were away and came home, I expected to see Snowball on the front steps. He would often be there when we drove into the driveway. I would tell Sylvester to keep looking for him too because one of these days he would be back.

Meanwhile the other white tomcat remained in the area. Rich said we were not going to feed any more strays and made me promise

Sylvester-looking inside Snowy's house for him.

not to encourage this one. I called him the imposter cat. It was very eerie how he showed up and seemingly impersonated Snowball. He knew all the spots and even befriended our cat Windy. I felt bad about feeding him that first day and then ignoring him when he came thereafter. Some would say God was answering my prayers by sending me another white cat. I just didn't feel that. I was more inclined to think of this as a trick of the devil to get me to accept less than what God had for me. I wanted *my* cat back, not just any white cat. I wonder how many times satan does that to each of us, tries to get us to accept less than the perfect thing God has for us. All we need to do sometimes is wait on God, but we get impatient and settle for less. God may have the perfect job or mate for us, but we can't wait and pick our own. How we short change ourselves. That's another lesson this whole incident taught me. It was much more than just about a missing cat. It became a huge faith ordeal for me. I really needed this to happen. I needed my cat back. I struggled with how easy this was for God to do, but He wasn't doing anything about it. The only good thing about the imposter cat being in the area was that every time I saw a white cat, my heart didn't skip a beat. I got used to seeing another white cat around.

I had a particularly rough morning on Saturday, March 22. It had been exactly one month since Snowball's disappearance. Not just any month but a very, very long and exhausting month. I cried. I prayed. I asked God to explain it all to me. Why? I just really wanted Snowball back. During the whole time that he was missing, Rich kept reinforcing the fact to me that Snowball wasn't that great of a pet. He couldn't understand why I wanted him back so badly. Why was it such a big deal? He thought I should just forget about him. I still believed Snowball would eventually come back, but on this specific day I just really missed him. Rich's evaluation of my missing friend was pretty accurate, so I pondered his question and wondered why I did miss the little guy so much. Here's what I came up with. For one thing, he was the softest animal I had ever touched. His pure white fur was so soft and fine and incredibly thick, he felt just like a stuffed animal when you held him. Our other cats had nice silky coats of fur, but nonetheless regular fur, not the wonderful texture of his. He would never let you hold him for long, but for the few minutes he did, he just sank into your arms, all squishy and soft. He was unique in that way. He had turned into a real roly-poly little guy, so there was a little more squish to him. I just wanted to hold him again. He had always been there and now he wasn't around. There was a real vacancy every time I went outside. That's the other reason why I wanted him back, to fill this void.

Chapter 4

Angels Among Us

Part of my morning routine is watching Joyce Meyer on television at 7:30 a.m. I believe she is one of the finest Bible teachers that exists today. Sometimes I eat breakfast and watch her or else I blast the TV so I can hear her while I'm getting ready for work. I rarely miss a program. It was Thursday, March 26. On this particular day, all I remember is her saying, **"Angels are ministering spirits sent to help us."** That is Biblically correct and a fact I believe very much. I think we'll all be surprised when we get to heaven and see all the situations angels helped us with and the trouble they helped us avoid. Anyhow, after hearing her say that, I said out loud, **"God please send my angel to get my cat and bring him home today."**

I teach only a morning class at the college, so I am home in the afternoon. It was around 3:00 p.m. (still March 26). Rich was outside doing something with his golf stuff in the trunk of his car and I was checking on how my flowers were doing. The imposter cat was in our backyard and then went two houses down to Nora's. I really didn't want any more stray cats calling my house their house, but there he was and no doubt he was hungry. Feeling sorry for him, I went inside to get him some food. Then I walked down to Nora's and put it under the bush where he was sitting. I did have to admit that it was nice not to have stray cats hanging all around. There had been two regular tomcats at the restaurant—LBC (little black cat) and Woolly Cat. Not long ago we had changed their food from grocery store cat food to the premium food, and since that time they had been only sporadic visitors.

The pet storeowner said the new food was the equivalent to what we would consider health food, which to them would have been a little less tasty. However, sometimes they would still be in the backyard sleeping (no doubt awaiting the return of the tasty stuff) and I would have to send them on their way before I took Sylvester out. Woolly Cat had gotten into a major fight with him a few summers ago, and with so many diseases around, you just never know what a stray will be carrying around with it. The same week Snowball disappeared was also to be the last time that I ever saw either one of them. For whatever reason (I'll never know) they felt it was time to move on. It was better this way with the restaurant closed and all the strays gone. I proceeded to talk to the imposter cat and told him that I once had a white cat sort of like him. I heard myself asking him if he would like to be my new Snowy, and then immediately retracting the statement and the thought. The real Snowy would be back. There was no need or desire for a replacement. That was that. I left him and I went back to whatever it was I was doing prior to his interrupting me.

Later in the same afternoon, about 5:00 p.m., I was in the kitchen making something for supper. I had to teach that night also, so I needed to eat and get ready. I looked out the kitchen window and saw the imposter cat all curled up in a ball in the backyard, looking very cute. Naturally he was in one of Snowball's favorite spots. I was just getting ready to summon Rich to look at him. Even though I knew it wasn't a good idea, I thought maybe if he saw how cute he was he might change his mind about our feeding him. However, before I could call Rich, I went speechless when I saw another white cat coming up the driveway and heading for the very spot the imposter cat was in! I called Rich and said that there were two white cats in the backyard! I then stated as a matter of fact, "***And I know that one is Snowball.***" I dashed outside and called him. Of course it was Snowball and he came over to us without hesitation. I was overjoyed to see him but not surprised. I had possessed this calm assurance inside me that he would be back.

And now he was. He was yowling, making a lot of noise, just like always. He was very thin, and so dirty he was not recognizable as being a white cat, plus he smelled very badly. He wanted to be petted and picked up. Ignoring the dirt and awful smell, I picked him up. There was nothing to him—just fur-covered bones. He wasn't very interested in food, but he was very thirsty. He was literally dying of thirst, as we would learn later. He had been missing for part or all of thirty-four days. Unfortunately, I couldn't spend much time with him because I had to get ready for work, but before I went back inside, I looked and he was in the restaurant eating. I knew I would see him in it again. When I left for work, he was sleeping in his house. Yep, I knew I'd see him in his house again. When I came home about 10:00 that night, he was on the front steps. That too, I knew. He was in all the places I had pictured him through the eye of faith, just as if he knew where he was supposed to be to complete the story.

There's faith that can move mountains and there's faith that can bring missing cats back—it's all really the same thing. As I said before, I'm not saying my faith is better than anybody else's, just better than mine had been. Fortunately God uses a variety of life's scenarios, even a missing cat, to grow us up spiritually. There's a bunch of stuff we as mere humans cannot do, and we can only rely on and believe that God can and will do it for us. I know He is willing to bless what is His, so we first need to make sure we belong to Him. At times you may wonder why this thing or that thing did or did not happen in your life. I have things I wonder about too. There are some things that no one has answers for. All I know for sure is that God can do what we cannot, and the ultimate decision is His.

Snowball came back on Thursday. We wanted to take him to the vet for a checkup to make sure he was okay, so on Friday I called to make an appointment. They had been previously all booked for the next two days, but the call just before mine had been a cancellation, so they could take him at 9:00 Saturday morning. Friday was also to be the beginning of new sleeping arrangements for Snowball. I couldn't bear the thought of him outside at night in such a weakened, vulnerable state, so we insisted he stay in the basement with Windy. We gave him a new bed that actually had been Sylvester's Christmas present. It had been slightly slept in only twice, because Sylvester decided he preferred sleeping with his people instead of in a boring cat bed. Snowball was so exhausted he didn't carry on as he previously did with his yowling, but rather just went to sleep. That is until Windy decided she wanted the new bed. Snowball was too tired to care and relocated himself to an old cat bed located under the steps on a shelf. Cats are such strange and funny little people.

Saturday morning arrived and Rich and I were in the waiting room at the veterinarian's office telling everyone about our cat that had been missing for thirty-four days. One lady asked what color he was. I said, "White." With a question in her voice she replied, "Oh, but not pure white?" I answered yes he was pure white, or rather he used to be. He was that dirty.

The vet shed some light as to what may have happened to him. He was extremely dehydrated which would account for his constant drinking of water. She said it appeared he had been trapped somewhere for the entire time. It had been an unusually rainy season, so if he was just lost he could have at least drunk rainwater—there were puddles everywhere. I surmised he had probably been trapped in a small area, which would account for his smelling like urine so badly. He weighed in at only nine pounds—his previous weight was fifteen pounds! He had lost over one third of his body weight. Fortunately, he was a bit on the plump side when he disappeared or else he may not have survived. Sadly, he lived off his own body fat for over a month. The poor little animal. I can't even begin to imagine what went through his mind. Day after day and night after night trapped somewhere. The days turned into weeks and the weeks into a month. Comparatively speaking, thirty-four days may not be that long of a time, but to an animal trapped without food or water it probably seemed like eternity. Snowball could have lasted only another day or two in his present condition.

In the flyer I distributed door to door, I had asked people to check their garages and storage areas for him. Maybe someone had left on vacation the day he disappeared. Sometimes in the winter people do go on vacation to the warmer climates for a month or longer. Pathetically, maybe someone just didn't care and couldn't be bothered over a cat. I guess we'll never know for sure what happened to him. The important thing is that he is back and relatively healthy. The vet said it would be best just to allow the dirt to wear off of him. That was a good idea because the last thing he needed was more trauma in his life in the form of a bath. When we returned home, I was able to clean him up a bit with wet paper towels. He was incredibly dirty and that worked fairly well. We also gave him vitamins to build his strength back up. He acted much friendlier, wanted more attention, and seemed to truly appreciate everything we were doing for him. We joked about how he had had a long time to think about how he had been acting and to mend his ways.

It is presently June. Snowball has been back for almost three months and is totally recovered. The wet paper towels and daily brushings did wonders. With warmer weather arriving, he has also shed his grimy winter coat and got a brand new coat for summer. He is once again pure white and a beautiful cat. However, the day I secured a possible publisher for his story, he came home filthy dirty. He had been rolling in dirt somewhere and even had mud caked on his head. I told him that was no way for the star of my story to look. He didn't understand. If he did understand he no doubt would have wished that there were no story—that this whole horrendous thing had never happened to him. We wish it hadn't happened either, but some good has come out of it, both for him and for us. The benefits for him are that he lives in the house now at night and during inclement weather. He's safe from all the strays that come out at night to do battle with each other. He's adjusted to this and we all sleep better knowing everyone is home safe. We benefit from his being a better pet and acting a bit more normally. He still has his wacky moments when he reverts to his old ways and becomes paranoid, but these incidents are becoming fewer and fewer. I'm confident that in time they will cease altogether. He'll spend much more time inside with us in the wintertime so more progress will be made in this area I'm sure. Sylvester is truly king of the house, so I don't know if the time will ever come when Snowy will be able to actually share the upstairs house with him. Time will tell. As for Windy, she is getting older, perhaps near eleven now, and is happy to visit us in the house and then go back to the basement to her new bed. Incidentally, we bought another bed for Snowball and threw the old one away, so they could both have new beds. They are side by side on the shelf under the basement steps and that is where they sleep at night. Aside from

Snowy & Windy—In their beds under the steps

swatting at each other from time to time, they are the best of pals. Sylvester neither likes nor dislikes either one of them, but rather tolerates them—sometimes. At times he thinks they should be swiftly chased back to wherever they came from. It's the hierarchical cat structure that he feels necessary to establish himself king of daily. Life goes on and is perfect in our three-cat household.

Chapter 5

What a Surprise!

To complete the story, I must tell you about one final incident that happened the last week in June. I had noticed blood coming from the gum area on one of Snowball's front teeth. June was Dental Awareness month for animals, and I had been bombarded with information about taking care of pet's teeth. My understanding is that the decay and bacteria can eventually cause more serious problems with the heart, liver, and other vital organs. So I was naturally concerned when I looked at his teeth and saw nothing but dark spots of tarter and inflamed looking gums. I made an appointment for him and Windy (since she was considered a senior cat citizen) at a local animal hospital that specialized in dentistry. Since dentistry involves anesthetizing the cat in order to perform the necessary procedures, the cat has to be checked for general healthiness first. Together they went in for the pre-treatment exam to see just what had to be done. On this particular day I was to receive a major and shocking surprise. It was the fact Snowball is much older than we had presumed him to be. I had thought he was about six or seven years old now, and had been telling him he was the 'baby' of the family. The vet said he is closer to twelve years old! She could tell by the geriatric changes in his teeth. His back teeth were severely decomposed and she said probably when she removed the tarter that several of them would just crumble from decay and need to be extracted.

The following week both Windy and Snowball went for their dental work. Windy just needed a cleaning and polishing. Snowball, on the other hand, had to have three teeth extracted. He had to have been in a great deal of pain. He appears to be a much happier cat now and his remaining teeth are pearly white when he smiles. I think he is slowly realizing that the temporary discomforts we put him through were really to help him.

For whatever reason his age was previously miscalculated and for that I am grateful. Had I known he was twelve years old, I probably would have thought he just wandered off to die someplace when he disappeared. The life span of an outside cat is about half of what it is for an indoor cat, usually only five to seven years. Snowball would have been well over his allotted time, so I would not have looked for him to the degree that I did. The faith and prayers, which I believe brought him home, would not have happened.

I would say Snowball has been very blessed with a long life as an outside cat. It's unfortunate, but when cats are allowed to roam freely outside they often meet up with premature deaths in the form of traffic accidents, diseases carried by other animals, or can encounter an array of other fatal mishaps. It's easy to say for the sake of safety that cats should be kept indoors, but when you take in strays such as Snowball, it is very difficult to get them to stay inside all day long when they have spent years outside. Whether or not to allow your cat access to the great outdoors is a tough decision every pet owner has to make. If you live in a very dangerous area, such as busy streets all around, then logically you must make the decision for your cat. Better an unhappy cat in the house than a dead cat outside.

In conclusion, I am not concerned about his age. It was a brief shock to have his age double before my very eyes—one minute he was six, the next he was twelve. However, I believe God will bless Snowball, Rich, and myself (and our other cats) with many more happy, healthy years together. Just recently *Cat Fancy* magazine had a contest for the oldest cat and dear sweet *Grandpa* checked in at thirty-three years old. That is a very ripe old age for a cat and I am believing for ages of at least twenty-five for our cats. Sadly, a few months later, they reported *Grandpa* dying on April 1, 1998.

I give God the glory and credit for bringing Snowball back. I remind Snowball regularly that when he was missing the Lord Jesus brought him home. I don't want him to become like the Israelites who were brought out of Egypt and then forgot who set them free. I realize, since he's a cat, he probably doesn't understand a word of it. In reality, in reminding him it is really myself that I am reminding to remember the goodness of our Lord. At one time in my life I did forget and had to be brought back too. I work hard at never allowing that happen again. I'm thankful that God allows something I hold dear (Snowball) to be used to help me remember from whence I came. I'll be forever grateful He brought us both back home.

End

Late Summer 1998

THE

END

Author's Personal Christian Testimony

My entire childhood was lived in Bessemer, a small town in western Pennsylvania, just minutes from the Ohio state line. I have no memories of not going to church as a child, but rather a series of meaningless ones from doing so. As a very small child I can remember the Bible characters *not* coming to life on the flannel board in the basement of the church during the Sunday School hour before the actual church service. Then, unequivocally, my most vivid memory would unfold once we were in the actual service. A series of well-meaning ladies would come and greet me with hugs and kind words and dote over me, presuming me to be such a darling little child. The problem I had with this welcoming group was trying not to suffocate as I held my breath so I did not have to breathe in their horrendous breath. It had the unmistakable smell of coffee, mixed with large doses of just awfulness, which totally nauseated me. As a child, I just assumed that this was what drinking coffee did to you, and to this day I do not, nor never have drunk coffee.

For whatever reason, my parents stopped going to church. As fate would have it, my best friend, Toni, lived in the corner house across the street from my church. She and I would go together and then I would walk home, it being less than a mile. In my child's mind I would ponder the great mysteries of the universe on this trek home. The most reoccurring subject, Sunday after Sunday, was just how good you had to be to get into heaven. Just how many times could I break things or eat all the cookies and blame it on my brother? Did God have a mysterious cut off number and if so, what was it? How could I be sure I was measuring up and would end up in heaven someday?

Later on when I was in high school my science teacher was also my Sunday School teacher. This was truly a surreal situation: on Sunday morning he would tell us about God creating mankind and the entire universe, and then on Monday in science class he would expound with animated fervor about the big bang theory of creation. To me, he gave the unmistakable impression that science was correct and the Bible was just well meaning stories that really should not be taken very seriously.

In my teenage years I continued faithfully to read my Bible before I went to bed. Being a product of the 60's, I couldn't help wondering if some of the writers had not been partakers of hallucinogenic drugs before they wrote some of the stuff. Be assured that they did not and that there are sensible explanations for every word in the Bible. But back then I did wonder.

Without giving you all the details of how I solitarily frequented various churches, listened to way-out religious people on the radio, and went by myself to Billy Graham type crusades, I will just sum it up by saying that God did finally send a very special person named Bill into my life to explain the simple plan of salvation to me. I learned from him that Christianity is not a religion but rather a personal relationship with God. We can not become good enough or worthy enough on our own to be accepted by God. Isaiah 64:6 states, "But we are all as an unclean *thing*, and all our righteousnesses *are* as filthy rags; and we all do fade as a leaf; and our iniquities, like the wind, have taken us away." Also Ephesians 2:8-9 emphasizes that, "For it is by grace you have been saved through faith—and this not from yourselves, it is the gift of God-—not by works, so that no one can boast." We cannot buy or work our way into heaven; we just have to accept what God has already provided for us through Jesus. I went to Mexico a few years ago and some of the people were so appreciative of what we did for them that they brought us their most prized possession or some special food treat. They were very poor, living in poverty and squalor; their treasures were junk to us. It made me think of the above scriptures. Our best, our self- righteousnesses are garbage to God. We, of course, accepted the Mexicans gifts humbly and gratefully so not to insult them, but God cannot accept us apart from Christ's finished work. Bill explained it to me in the following way and I would like to, in turn, explain it to you.

Mankind is created as a triune being. There is a physical part to us, which is the body we live in; we have a soul, commonly accepted to mean our mind, will, and emotions; and thirdly the spirit element. In the third chapter of the book of Genesis, when the serpent tempts Eve with the forbidden fruit in the Garden of Eden, she repeats God's strict admonition to him, "You must not eat fruit from the tree that is in the middle of the garden, and you must not touch it, or you will die." The serpent retorts, "You will not surely die." They did indeed eat it and did not die, so was the serpent (Satan) correct and God lied? As a child on my walks home I also pondered this. Now I know the truth. Actually, they did die—spiritually. When Jesus speaks of being born again in the third chapter of John, he is speaking of our spirit, the part of us capable of communicating with God, being made alive or being reborn. When that happens we are once again totally alive and functioning as God originally intended for us to live. He is then able to start communicating with us and molding us into the person He created us to be. Our dead spirit has been resurrected. How does this happen? How does a person become born again, or become spiritually alive? First we must acknowledge that we are sinners. Romans 6:23 states, "For all have sinned and fall short of the glory of God." Then we must realize that in our present state we have a death sentence hanging over us which results in eternal separation from God. Romans 6:23 sums this up by saying, "For the wages of sin is death, but the gift of God is eternal life in Christ Jesus our

Lord." God came to our rescue by sending Jesus to become our substitute in paying our sin debt; that was the purpose of Him dying on the cross. "But God demonstrates his own love for us in this: While we were still sinners, Christ died for us."-- Romans 5:8. Our part in this is just to accept the gift, just as you accept a Christmas or birthday gift. You do this by asking Jesus to come into your life and cleanse you from sin and make you into the person He would have you be. Romans 10:9-10 pretty much states the way. It says, "That if you confess with your mouth, 'Jesus is Lord,' and believe in your heart that God raised Him from the dead, you will be saved. For it is with your mouth that you confess and are saved." You may or may not "feel" any different. You believe that God has accepted you and given you eternal life by faith. Hebrews 11:1 says, "Now faith is being sure of what we hope for and certain of what we do not see." If you have not had this experience and would like to do so, pray the following prayer:

Dear God, I believe Jesus is the holy Son of God. I believe that He died on the cross for my sins and He rose from the dead. Jesus, I now confess that you are my Savior. I ask you to wash all my sins away and make me a child of God. I give my life totally to you today. Amen

Please feel free to contact me if you have any questions concerning your new life in Christ. May God truly bless you and may you enjoy His best all your life.

Sandra Harknett
SLHarknett@aol.com

ORDER FORM TO OBTAIN ADDITIONAL BOOKS
Only Personal Checks or Money Orders Accepted/ No Credit Cards or Cash

SHIP TO:	NAME		
	ADDRESS		
	CITY		
	STATE		
	ZIP		
HOW MANY	PRICE EACH	NAME OF BOOK	PRICE
	$12.99	Just Four Cats	
		Postage	$3.00
		Tax	
		TOTAL	

Mail To: Sandra Harknett
102 Cleveland Ter
Bloomfield, NJ 07003

ORDER FORM TO OBTAIN ADDITIONAL BOOKS
Only Personal Checks or Money Orders Accepted/ No Credit Cards or Cash

SHIP TO:	NAME		
	ADDRESS		
	CITY		
	STATE		
	ZIP		
HOW MANY	PRICE EACH	NAME OF BOOK	PRICE
	$12.99	Just Four Cats	
		Postage	$3.00
		Tax	
		TOTAL	

Mail To: Sandra Harknett
102 Cleveland Ter
Bloomfield, NJ 07003